The Valeron Code

The Valeron code was simple: 'Trust in the Lord, but keep a gun handy.' And when it came to harming one of them or their family, they had but one commandment: 'Thou shalt not get away with it'!

Rodney (Lightning Rod) Mason had a habit of getting involved in other people's problems. So when a banker hires him to help his sister, it seems just another job. But Rod finds more than he bargained for in Deliverance, Colorado. The opposition is ruthless and the victim is someone who can change his world.

When an ambush leaves Rod vulnerable and unable to fight back, word is sent to his brother and cousins. Within hours, Wyatt and Jared Valeron are dispatched to aid their kin. The odds against them mount, but a Valeron doesn't know how to quit. A final showdown will decide who lives, who dies . . . and how the Valeron family code works.

The Valeron Code

Terrell L. Bowers

A Black Horse Western

ROBERT HALE

ISBN 978-0-7198-2065-6

The Crowood Press
The Stable Block
Crowood Lane
Ramsbury
Marlborough
Wiltshire SN8 2HR

www.bhwesterns.com

Robert Hale is an imprint
of The Crowood Press

Typeset by
Derek Doyle & Associates, Shaw Heath
Printed and bound in Great Britain by
CPI Group (UK) Ltd, Croydon, CR0 4YY

CHAPTER ONE

Tommy Smith, although only seventeen, held his ground, as Lynette Brooks stood at his side. The pair of men facing them were Sandoval and Connor, two toughs who worked for Mayor Lafferty. The mayor was in cahoots with Rutherford and Gilmore, the banker and saloon owner, who pretty much controlled everything that happened in Deliverance, Colorado.

'You've been printing some unflattering things in your news rag, woman,' Sandoval threw out the accusation. 'Casting slanderous attacks against our law-abiding citizenry don't look good to the people passing through. Some potential buyers of business property or farmland might be put off by your writing. Can't have you destroying the reputation of our fair town.'

'That's right,' Connor joined in. 'Name calling is a crime.'

'It's only slander when it isn't the truth,' Lynette countered.

Connor frowned, uncertain what slander meant. He looked at his partner for assistance, as he was the brighter of the two.

'You think, because you're wearing a skirt, we won't teach you a lesson,' Sandoval sneered. 'Well, you best be thinking again.'

'You tell her, pard.'

'Bet you'd look real purty dressed in a coat of hot tar with a feather overcoat,' the menacing Sandoval continued. 'I knew a feller who had that done to him – took a month before he got all the black off. He lost most of his hide getting the chore done.'

Tommy anchored his jaw, speaking through clenched teeth. 'What kind of men are you, threatening a genteel woman and editor of the town's newspaper?'

'We're the kind who sets down the rules and enforces the law!' Sandoval declared. 'You'd best keep your trap shut, pup . . . or we'll close it for you.'

Lynette fumed. 'How dare you threaten my assistant. You are nothing more than hired bullies for Harve Rutherford and his partners in crime. I intend to print the truth about you – all of you!'

'Then you're gonna do it without any help,' Sandoval jeered. Aggressively, he shoved Tommy hard enough that the youth backed up several steps. Before he could catch his balance, the man strode forward and clouted him hard alongside the head. The sudden punch stunned Tommy and he had no chance to defend himself.

Lynette screamed at him to stop as Connor joined in. The two men began to hit Tommy from either side. Rushing forward, Lynette grabbed hold of Connor's arm, but he whirled about and shoved her to the ground. Tommy was pummelled unmercifully until he collapsed in a heap. Lying helpless and dazed, Sandoval kicked him in the ribs. Lynette scrambled to her feet as both assailants kicked Tommy several times.

Frantic to stop the beating, Lynette pushed between the two men and dropped to her knees. She threw her arms around Tommy to protect him from the two vicious goons. Her action stopped the attack, but Sandoval spat a stream of tobacco juice on to the ground next to her.

'Write about this in your newspaper,' Sandoval growled, hovering over her, 'and we'll be back to finish this!'

'Like my pal says,' Connor confirmed.

'You're both animals!' Lynette cried. 'Disgusting, inhuman animals!'

Sandoval chuckled at her outburst, but was deadly serious when he spoke again.

'You best listen to what we're telling you, you ink-slinging troublemaker! If you want to keep printing your newspaper, you'll start writing stories that Mayor Lafferty and our other prominent citizens like to read. Otherwise, female or not, we're gonna ride you out of town on a rail!'

Lynette grabbed Tommy under his armpits and helped him to stand up. He managed the feat with a Herculean effort, but was barely conscious. He folded at the middle and spat out a mouthful of blood. Unable to maintain his balance, he sagged heavily against her.

'You two cowards are the ones who deserve to be tarred and feathered!' she avowed.

Sandoval raised a hand to dismiss her protest. 'Heed what we say, woman. Next time it will be more than a bruise or two.'

'I'm taking Tommy to Doctor Wight. If you've seriously

hurt him, I'll see you both behind bars!'

The bully ignored her feeble threat and tugged on Connor's arm. 'Let's go get some coffee and a fresh roll at the bakery. These here law-officer-type chores sure do work up an appetite.'

The two of them laughed and sauntered up the street.

Lynette helped Tommy stagger to the doctor's office. Of all the people in Deliverance, the doctor was clinically unbiased, treating every person in town as a potential patient.

Appraising the youth's bruised and bleeding face, she grit her teeth and seethed with rancor. What could a lone woman do against a town full of tyrants and ruffians? Her parents were dead and her only brother worked in a bank back in Nebraska. She had invested every dime she had in a Washington Hand Press and printing equipment so she could start her own newspaper. The sales, subscribers and advertising earned her enough to get by . . . or had, until Rutherford and his band of coyotes came to town. Within a few months, they had assumed the bank, the main saloon and manoeuvred to gain control of nearly every business in town. The bank also held deeds on most of the nearby farms and small ranches. Her telling the truth about the malignant tyrant, Rutherford, and his henchmen had earned her powerful enemies and a steep rise in the rent for her office and one room apartment. She wanted to fight the good fight, to be a spokesperson for the downtrodden populace, but she was nearly broke and had no way to physically combat these men. How could she continue to print the truth without some kind of help or assistance?

Rodney Mason sat on the inside of his cell, playing a game of checkers with the town deputy. He and the lawman were friends, but an altercation between Mason and a couple of hunters had landed him in jail. It was his move when the door to the sheriff's office opened.

A bespectacled young man, likely in his early twenties, entered the room. He was dressed like a dude stumping for an election to office, complete with a city-slicker tie and ruffled white shirt. He was lean of build and stood about five-and-a-half feet tall, not including the funny-looking derby hat atop his neatly-shorn head.

'I'm Richard Brooks,' he announced. 'Marshal Konrad Ellington said I could find a man by the name of Rod Mason here.'

'You've found him,' the deputy said, standing up to meet the fellow.

'You're Mason?'

The deputy hooked his thumb at the prisoner. 'He is.'

Richard's jaw dropped at the news. He stared at the two of them, perplexed, before asking the obvious question. 'He's a prisoner?'

'Happens sometimes when you have a strict judge,' the deputy replied. 'You want a word with him? He sure ain't going nowhere.'

The young fellow shook his head. 'But I need his help! Marshal Ellington said he was the best man for the job.'

'Speak up, buster,' Mason growled. 'I've got the deputy backed up for the kill here. You best not be spoiling my game unless this is durned important.'

'It is!' Richard declared. 'My sister's newspaper is in dire trouble. The rent for her building has doubled over the past few months, there are unwarranted taxes strangling the citizens, and her apprentice was beaten almost to death last week. The culprits are several tyrants and a couple of rowdy town bullies who run the law! It is my duty as her brother to help her resolve the situation.'

'And Konrad sent you to find me?'

'He said you were the best man for the job,' he repeated. Then, with a queer look, 'He didn't say you were a convict serving time.'

The deputy moved the table and checkerboard, then used his foot to shove the chair toward the newcomer. 'Here you go, young fella,' he said. 'I've got a couple chores to do. I'll leave the two of you alone for a few minutes.' Then with a smirk at Mason, 'We'll call the game a draw.'

Mason glowered at the newcomer. 'Thanks, buster. You just cost me two bits!'

Richard took a long look at Mason. He saw a rather large-boned man – six-foot tall, a sturdy 190 pounds, with a battle-worn face and flinty eyes that bore the history of many conflicts. Unshaven for at least a week, with unruly hair that nearly reached his shoulders, the man in the cell looked more a wild man than an infrequent deputy US Marshal.

'Marshal Ellington said you are known as "Lightning Rod" Mason,' Richard said at length.

'Was a time in my youth when I was accused of having a short fuse,' he replied. 'The nickname kind of stuck.'

'Marshal Ellington also said you are very good with a gun.'

'There's been times I was forced to defend myself

during a lively exchange.'

'And Marshal Ellington said you once engaged in pugilism for a living.'

'Only fought in the ring for a short while.' Mason shrugged. 'Man gets hungry, he does whatever it takes to earn a meal.' Then with a scowl: 'Anything else Marshal Ellington had to say?'

Richard flinched, but smiled weakly. He pulled the chair closer to the cell and sat down astraddle. 'Did I mention he said you were the best man for the task ahead?'

'Yeah, I heard that part. What kind of task?'

'I want you to teach me how to defend myself.'

Mason frowned. 'Defend yourself? From whom?'

Richard related the story of how a despot was harassing his sister and two men had beaten her assistant so badly that he nearly died from the injuries. He said the place was Deliverance, Colorado, and several men had showed up a few months back and took over the town. The main culprit now owned the bank; a second ended up with the primary saloon; and the third took over as mayor. The mayor also had a couple toughs who ran roughshod over everyone in the valley. According to her letter, the trio was taxing the populace to poverty and were about to run her out of business. Next he explained what he wanted.

After listening to his tale, Mason shook his head. 'So you expect me to teach you to fight so you can go make things right for your sister?'

'Yes, I'll need to apprehend the men responsible for the attack on her printer's apprentice and turn them over to the US Marshal.'

'After that, I suspect you intend to help your sister run her newspaper?'

'Oh, heavens no!' He puffed up his chest like a bantam rooster. 'I'm vice president at the Merchants' Bank of Omaha. I took a leave of absence for thirty days to deal with this issue.'

Mason laughed. 'Thirty days? I couldn't make a fighting man out of you in a single month.'

Richard skewed his expression. 'You misunderstand. I must be back at my desk and working within the time frame – twenty-five days, actually. It's taken me nearly a week to find my way here.'

'It's a couple of days' ride to Deliverance. When you allow for your return to Omaha, you haven't got but a mere two weeks.'

'Well, I allowed for one week of training and another week to settle things for my sister.'

Richard did not hide his amazement. 'Got to hand it to you, buster, you don't lack for confidence.'

'When can you start?'

'I didn't say I'd take the job.'

'Marshal Ellington assured me that you would have his full support. Plus, I will give you a hundred dollars for the training and pay your fine so you can get out of here.'

Mason groaned. 'Did you tell Konrad your plans? I mean the part about you learning to fight so you could clean up a crooked town all by yourself?'

'Not in so many words,' Richard admitted. 'I told him the situation and he suggested I find you.'

'Good old Konrad,' Mason said dryly. *He expects I'll wet*

nurse this babe in the wilderness, then go and maybe get myself killed trying to help him. Strange, I thought we were friends.

Lynette was busy setting print when the door opened. She looked over her shoulder and ceased working. Dealer Gilmore was standing there, his moderately handsome face displaying both warmth and yearning.

'You're an amazing woman, Lynn,' he opened the conversation. Disregarding her dislike of the use of the pet name, he sedately continued. 'Your apprentice gets busted up and you proceed without so much as a deep breath.'

'I suppose you came to gloat about how your two brutes managed to beat up a boy half their age and size!'

'Actually, that was Rutherford's doing,' Dealer replied, continuing to eye her like a prize heifer at an auction. 'I spoke to him about the incident with your assistant and would like to square things so you don't go broke.'

'Oh?'

'Yes. Harve agreed to let you skip the rent this month.' Dealer shrugged. 'Seems you are three weeks behind already.'

'That's very generous of him . . . considering he has upped the rent to double what I was paying since he took control of the bank.'

'There are better and safer ways to make a living,' Dealer said. 'All you have to do is stop maligning those of us who moved here a few months back.'

'You mean to stop printing the truth about a bunch of scavengers who moved in and took over a wonderful little settlement? Who then turned it into a hostile environment where you control everyone and everything?'

'Every town is regulated by a few of its citizens. This is no different.'

'What happened to the banker, Mr Walters?' she questioned him. 'And how did you convince Mr McDowell to sell you his saloon?'

Dealer grinned. 'They saw no future in staying here. We paid them handsomely to search for greener pastures elsewhere.'

'And the new taxes and higher interest rates? I would think you make enough money fleecing drunks and gamblers without taking every cent the rest of us earn.'

'Gotta have civic improvements,' he said easily. 'And Harve has to make a profit to keep the bank in operation.'

'I'm sure he can barely scrape by, charging twenty-five to thirty per cent on his loans!'

'It's only business.' Another smirk. 'We do the best we can.' Before she could continue the debate, Dealer drew out a wad of bills from his pocket. He peeled off a couple and tossed them on to the counter. 'Here's thirty dollars to cover the loss of your help for the past couple weeks.' He winked at her. 'Take some time and think about your situation.'

'You mean my opposition to you and your dictator partner?'

Dealer relaxed his posture. 'You're an intelligent, fine looking woman, Lynn. Once you decide to stop fighting us, you and I could have something special together.'

'Special? You mean like sharing a bout of cholera or smallpox?'

He laughed. 'If you were my girl, I'd help your newspaper grow. How'd you like to have a readership that

covered the whole county? Maybe even develop a following in a few of the larger cities?'

'All it takes is the filthy money earned at the expense
of honest people you men have driven out of business or
from their homes.'

His lips curled in a sly grin. 'You keep throwing out
accusations you can't prove. We've done nothing illegal.'

'Because you scare everyone off with your gunmen.
Those who try to fight you end up dead or like Tommy –
isn't that what you mean?'

'I'm saying you needn't risk losing your business.
Cooperate. Allow me to come courting. It would make
everything so much better . . . for you and your newspaper.'

'It's very gracious of you to worry about my future.'

'I'm concerned for your safety as well,' he said, doing
little to conceal a threat. 'Harve will only take so much
before he strikes back.'

'You claim that you and Mr Rutherford don't break
the law,' she countered fiercely. 'So why should I fear
him?'

'The mayor and judge have denounced your articles
as propaganda against the growth and well-being of our
fair city. A newspaper can't survive without selling what
they write to customers.'

'So now you threaten the youngsters who sell my
papers on the street?'

'There might be some added pressure for people not
to buy the papers in the first place,' he stated meaningfully. 'Think about it, Lynn.'

Her eyes burned hot. 'You have no right to call me by

my first name, Dealer Gilmore. You are as responsible as Sandoval and Connor for Tommy's beating. He almost died from his injuries!'

'Buy yourself something nice with the money,' Dealer replied, ignoring her outburst. 'And give some thought to what I've said. You can earn a good living here in Deliverance. Just curb your poison pen and be civil towards me. I'd hate to see you lose everything you own, just so's you can malign me and my partner's reputation.'

'You can't buy or scare me, Mr Gilmore.'

Dealer displayed a vulgar sneer. 'You're too young and nubile to waste what's left of your life covering yourself in ink and writing trash, Lynn.' He purposely accented the moniker. It was a subtle demonstration of her lack of recourse to whatever he and Rutherford did or said. 'Give it some thought.'

Remaining outwardly calm, she said: 'Please leave. I have work to do.'

Dealer stared at her, not trying to hide his salacious hunger for her. After a few seconds he lifted a hand in farewell and went out the door. Once alone, Lynette nearly collapsed from the strain. Her knees were shaking and her heart was pounding hard enough to crack a rib. She managed to control her trembling long enough to pick up the money. It was enough to pay the doctor for treating Tommy and also the week's wages she owed the young man. He claimed he had wanted to come back to work for her, but his family feared retribution and had demanded he quit. She couldn't blame them. Tommy's life was worth more than a few lines in a newspaper, especially when there was nothing anyone could do about the situation.

Lynette had grown resilient and independent while helping to raise her brother. The one man in her life had turned out to be a rogue who swept her off of her feet, used her to suit his purpose, then dropped her in the gutter. He ruined her reputation and left her too ashamed to trust another man. Dealer was cut from the same cloth as that deceitful, womanizing cur. He didn't want a woman as a companion or partner in life, he wanted her for his personal satisfaction, a trophy to show off until he tired of her. Unfortunately, rejecting Dealer only inspired him to try harder. That he was ten years older than her did not matter, he ran the biggest saloon for miles around and considered his position as grounds for a romance.

Before she could ponder her predicament further, the office door opened a second time. It was Peter, one of the youths who sold papers for her each week. He also worked as a town runner. He was in his early teens and did about any job that would earn him a few cents. He walked up to the small counter and flashed a wide grin.

'Hey, Miss Brooks!' he greeted. Then he held out a piece of paper from his pocket. 'This here just come for you. It arrived special at the telegraph office. The sender paid extra for fast, personal delivery, so I brought it straight away.'

She took the message and offered him a smile. 'Thank you, Peter.'

He laughed. 'No, thank you! The sender of this here wire done paid an extra fifty cents for seeing you got this straightaway.'

She thanked him again anyway, as he whirled about and went out the door. She didn't watch after him, but put her attention on the folded piece of paper. It was a communication from her brother. She had mentioned Tommy being beaten in her last letter. It was a surprise to hear from him so soon, especially by telegraph. He said for her not to worry, that he was on his way. He promised to handle things and see everything was settled before he left.

Thinking of Richard, she was overtaken with incredulity. Her brother was very good with numbers and had worked himself up from bank clerk and teller to the position of vice president. She recalled her last visit with him, before she had used all of her money to leave that city behind and seek her destiny further west. Richard lived in a small house like a chipmunk in a burrow, seldom peeking out of his hole except to buy a few groceries. As a youth, he was picked on for being small and bookish. Timid was not a strong enough word for him. He avoided any manner of conflict and had never learned to fight or shoot a gun. He would be completely out of his element if he showed up and tried to lock horns with the hard-case sorts Rutherford and Dealer had on their payroll.

'Richard,' she murmured aloud. 'I love you dearly, but you are not up to something like this. I pray you don't come here and end up like Tommy . . . or worse!'

CHAPTER TWO

Richard stood with his arms hanging limply at his sides, gasping for air, his chest heaving from the vigorous exertion.

'Look, dummy,' Mason criticized him. 'You've got no power to your punches. When you hit a man, it has to be hard enough to scramble his wits. If you don't put him down with a few well-chosen licks, he'll come back at you and do some damage of his own.'

'I'm hitting the punching bag – mattress – whatever this wadded-up thing is.' He gasped before finishing. 'I'm done. Exhausted. I can't even lift my arms!'

'I chose this bag because your hands are soft. I prefer a sack of grain, because that toughens your knuckles too. You might not have time to put on a pair of gloves. You have to protect your hands.'

'But what's with this jabbing stuff?' Richard complained. 'Simply sticking a fist in the other guy's face won't knock him off of his feet.'

'A jab keeps your opponent off balance, so he can't set himself to knock you flat. You poke him between the eyes or in the nose hard enough that he can't see your next punch coming. That's when you bust his chops and lay him out on the ground.'

Richard stood before Mason, chest heaving to regain his wind, with his hands on his hips. 'This is a total waste of time. I thought you were going to teach me to—'

Without warning, Mason launched a sharp left jab to Richard's breastbone. It knocked his feet out from under him and he landed on his rump. It took a few seconds before he could catch his breath. Then he began to rub his chest.

'Holy Hannah! That hurt!'

Mason glowered down at him. 'Imagine that mild tap hitting you in the nose. You would be totally exposed and helpless when I unleashed a roundhouse and knocked you heels-over-shoulders flat on your face. The fight would be over.'

'B-but, how do you manage to get that much power behind such a short poke?'

'By doing just what I've been teaching you to do.'

Richard slowly got to his feet. He continued to rub the tender spot as he regarded Mason with a narrow appraisal. 'How long did it take you to acquire such a great deal of force for your "mild tap"?'

'I worked at it for several months, all the time I was fighting with the carnival.'

'Then I say we forgo these lessons. We need to get going. I've wasted two days and learned nothing . . . other than not to engage in fisticuffs.'

Mason sighed in agreement. 'All right, buster. We'll start out first thing in the morning. Let's go down to the general store and pick up the supplies we'll need. You can buy an extra hundred rounds of ammo so we can practice your shooting each night.'

'A hundred rounds?'

'I use that much every month. Usually twice that. You don't get good at something unless you practice.'

'I'm for a bath to soak my aching muscles.' He looked at Mason.

'Wouldn't hurt you to also get a bath, haircut and shave.'

'What for?'

'So you don't frighten my sister when she gets a look at you.'

'It doesn't sound like we are heading for a beauty contest.'

'Funny you should mention that. My sister actually won a contest at a local fair once, for being the most attractive girl, back when we were still living at home. I also won a first-place ribbon – it was a math competition.'

'The only math you should be concerned with is how many men in Deliverance will be pitted against the two of us.'

'According to one of Lynette's letters, it's mainly the banker, mayor, a saloon owner and their hired men. Unfortunately, by virtue of holding the deeds, they control most of the farms, ranches and businesses in the valley.'

'Could be, your sister's on a fool's errand. Why on earth does she insist on bucking such high odds with no chance of winning?'

'Lynette is not your usual damsel in distress,' Richard answered. 'She has a dogged determination to try and right wrongs when she sees them. Even when we were both living at home, she was always taking up for some social cause – you know, underpaid workers, indentured help, even the poor treatment of prisoners at the local jail. I lost count of how many times we got a rock through our window or a warning letter on our doorstep. I admit, I was relieved when she finally left. It allowed me to live in peace.'

'And now you're riding to her rescue like a big brother should.'

Richard chuckled. 'Yeah, she'll probably get a laugh out of that. Being three years older than me, she was the one who had to stick up for me growing up.'

'Circumstances would suggest you have picked a one-sided fight to prove your manhood to your sister.'

Richard took on a serious mien. 'I want to thank you for joining me, Mason. I am candidly aware of my lack of abilities when it comes to a fight. I've never even hit another person in anger before. I doubt I'll be much help.'

'If Konrad wanted you to take me along, he likely knew the odds and the troubles we were going to find. Let's hope you can learn to shoot. It sounds like we're headed to a place where I will need someone backing my play.'

'I'll do my very best,' Richard vowed.

His promise didn't lessen Mason's concern. Facing a host of powerful men didn't sound like a walk through a wheat field. Konrad had once told him he was the most able man he'd ever hired. Well, this time he might be in over his head.

Harve Rutherford ordered his housekeeper to bring out a couple glasses of apple brandy and took a chair on the veranda. There was a small table with several chairs along the wall of the house. Sometimes he and Dealer would have a couple of his men or guests over to play cards, when the weather was comfortable for sitting outside. The roof over the porch had been added after he took possession of the house. He enjoyed his position as king, the ultimate ruler of an entire town.

'It's been a good few months,' he said to the mayor. 'We've gained control of this valley and are in a good position to make a lot of money. There's plenty of traffic from travellers, a main stage route going in three different directions, and the possibility of getting a rail spur to the mainline of the Union Pacific railroad. Everything is going our way.'

'Yeah,' Lafferty agreed. 'Most everyone has fallen in line, other than the woman editor.'

'Dealer is hot on her heels.' Rutherford uttered a grunt. 'As if the Brooks woman would ever let him touch her.'

Lafferty agreed. 'She's pretty high and mighty. Don't scare for nothing either.'

'I don't like to shut down our only newspaper, but that unmanageable wildcat is making a real nuisance of herself.'

Lafferty didn't speak, as the housekeeper brought out two drinks. (She was an elderly widow with no family, so she had taken on the chore of a live-in cook and house-keeper.) He took a sip and enjoyed the coolness of the drink. He envied Rutherford and Dealer, who lived with as much luxury as could be bought. They had added an ice house out back of their two-story dwelling that provided them with cold drinks year around. He often resented being a third wheel, not involved in the decision-making or overall profit from their mutual endeavours. However, Dealer and Rutherford ran the gang, always had. He had to be satisfied with the position they gave him, and being mayor of the town paid well, without a lot of physical work.

'I never was much for apple jack,' he told Rutherford, 'but serving it cold . . . by Jingo!, that hits the spot.'

'Money has its advantages.'

'Dealer seems to be doing well at the saloon too.' Lafferty snorted.

'Yeah, you fellows sure know how to take charge of a town.'

'Dealer only has one weakness,' Rutherford criticized. 'He never saw a pretty woman he didn't want for himself. His interest in our lady editor is the only reason she isn't gone.'

'Got to admit, she's a cut above most daisies.' He gulped and hurried to say, 'Still, she's a real pest when it comes to writing those stinkin' newspaper articles.'

Rutherford got down to business. 'What's the latest on her?'

The mayor twitched. 'I stopped by the newspaper office, but she refused to talk to me. She was busy setting print. Looks as if she's going to put out her weekly paper on schedule.'

'Your two chowder-head flunkeys didn't do one bit of good. Beating up her apprentice only makes us look like bullies.'

'Sandoval and Connor did what they could. You said not to hurt the woman, so they put the kid out of action for a couple weeks.' He added: 'It worked a little, 'cause his folks made him quit.'

Rutherford did not let up. 'I pay you well to handle these kinds of things. It doesn't look good for me and the bank, her bashing me in every edition for gouging people on interest or foreclosing on farmers. Something has to be done.'

'If need be,' Lafferty lowered his voice, 'we can arrange for a fire. A little lamp oil, a match – we can burn the building down around her ears.'

'Not yet, Mike. But it might come to that.' Rutherford then put a curious look on him. 'You made this visit for a reason. What's on your mind?'

'A second telegraph message arrived a couple days ago from Lynette Brook's brother. It could be why she ain't packing her belongings. He is on his way here.' With a serious expression, 'He said he was going to "help her" with her problems.'

'I thought her brother worked in a bank, back east or the like?'

'Yes, his first wire came from Omaha. I believe that's where he lives. However, this second wire was sent from Denver.'

'A bank clerk shouldn't pose much of a problem.'

'No, sir,' Lafferty agreed. 'Even so, I wanted you to be

aware of what is going on . . . in case we have to deal with the guy.'

'Maybe he'll be smart and take his sister back with him to Omaha.'

'You want for us to give the editor another push, before he gets here?'

Rutherford rubbed his brow in thought. 'A little encouragement might not hurt, but remind your men not to do her physical harm. Have them make the point – we're running out of patience. Whenever her brother does arrive, you make sure he feels unwelcome too.'

'I'll see to it.'

Rutherford finished his drink and got to his feet. It forced Lafferty to do the same. Then the man placed his empty glass on the table and headed back to Main Street.

Watching him go, the bank owner ground his teeth. Why was it so few men could handle a job that needed a little ordinary logic? Perhaps the saying was wrong. From the people he'd encountered there were very few men with the ability to think and act rationally and appropriately to any given situation.

'Ought to rename it "rare sense",' he muttered. 'There sure isn't all that much common sense around these days.'

Teaching a dog to dance on stilts would have been a breeze compared to trying to make a marksman out of Richard. He had no coordination, lacked the eyesight for a shot at anything more than thirty feet away, and – seeking speed – he kept pulling the trigger before he was ready.

'What can I do?' he lamented. 'I can't seem to get everything to work in the right order.'

'Best advice: use what little coordination you have to duck quick and find cover,' Mason told him curtly.

'When you do it, it seems so easy. You just draw and shoot. Bam! You hit the target every time.' He uttered a deep sigh of regret. 'Even when I get the gun out and try to take aim, the bullet goes flying off to who knows where! I tell you, Mason, it's extremely depressing.'

'We agree on that much.'

'What are we going to do?'

Mason decided they had practised long enough. 'We're going to have something to eat and hit the blankets for the night. At the next town or trading post, we'll pick you up a double-barrel shotgun and head for Deliverance.'

'Is that easier to shoot – a shotgun?'

'It has more of a kick, buster, but you only have to point the barrel in the right direction. Even if you don't hit anything, the sight of one makes your adversary downright skittish.'

'Think we'll make it to Deliverance by tomorrow night?'

'We should get there by early afternoon. I reckon you and your sister will be reminiscing by suppertime.'

'I haven't seen her since she got mixed up with a wandering gambler,' Richard admitted. 'He treated her badly and I don't think she ever got past it. Anyway, I was too busy working to spend much time with her.' As they started the walk back to camp, he narrated how their folks had been poor. His father worked at a tannery and barely paid the bills. When his wife passed, his own health turned bad. He followed their mother to the grave a few months later.

'Lynette had enough schooling that she began to teach the local kids. It didn't pay much and I went to work at sixteen so we could keep our house. A year or so later, I landed a job at the bank. Soon as I was able to pay my own way, Lynette sold all of our folk's possessions, bought herself a printing press, and left town. We write back and forth all the time, but I haven't seen her in three years.'

'How come you haven't found a girl for yourself?'

'I've just attained a position of some importance. I wanted to be a good provider – no worrying about being able to afford food and clothing. You know?'

'Makes sense.'

'Soon as I buy myself a nice house, I'll start looking for an eligible lady. When and if I do marry, I'm going to be a better provider than my father.'

'Sounds like he did the best he could.'

'He did, but I want some of the finer things – indoor plumbing, a modern cooking stove, that sort of thing. I don't want my wife to die of old age at forty-one like my mother.'

'Seems like a good plan.'

'What about you?' he asked. 'Don't you want a home, a wife, and maybe a few kids?'

'I've only got one brother, but we're related to a big family named Valeron on my mother's side. My brother, Cliff, he went to work for our uncles, while I've been busy drifting around from one job to another. Besides, what kind of woman would want a man like me?'

'With your hair trimmed and having shaved off all of the unsightly facial hair, you are hardly in the category of an ogre.'

'A what?'

'You know, a monster, one whose scary features frighten children. Cleaned up the way you are, you look like a normal guy.'

'You saying I'm not normal otherwise?'

Richard swallowed a lump, as if fearful he had insulted a man who could use him as a dust cloth . . . and the present wilderness offered up a lot of dirt!

'Uh, n-no,' he stammered. 'You're as normal as me.'

Mason chuckled, having been teasing. 'You might not realize it, but that last remark is more of an insult than the first!'

Richard understood the jest and laughed with relief.

Lynette summoned her bravado as Sandoval and Connor moved to prevent her from reaching her office. She cringed inwardly at the sight of the pair, the very men who had beaten Tommy so savagely he had almost died.

'You're blocking the walkway,' she informed them curtly.

The twosome leered indolently at her, contented to remain in her path.

Lynette's heart began to race and she could not help feeling threatened. What would she do if they decided to molest her in some way? No one in town dared stand up to Lafferty or his two thugs.

'What do you want?' she demanded in a voice that belied her fear. Sandoval displayed an innocent expression. 'We don't want a thing, woman,' he said. 'But we're downright disappointed to see you're still printing scandalous venom about the mayor, Dealer and Rutherford in your newspaper. We must not have made ourselves clear the last time we visited.' A sneer broadened his thick lips. 'You remember, back when you had that young pup pretending to be a man at your side?'

'You had to know my report would be critical of your behaviour concerning such an unwarranted attack. If either of you ignorant buffoons could read, you would have probably enjoyed seeing your name in print!'

'Woman's got a tongue that could strip bark from a tree,' Sandoval remarked to his sidekick. 'You think God really give it some thought before He allowed women should be able to speak?'

Connor shook his head. 'Real shame He made some females so gal-durn purty.'

'Probably did that so's a man would put up with their barbed tongue and endless nagging.'

'You're right about that, pard.'

'Maybe the lady needs some help and is too proud to ask for it,' Sandoval said, displaying a twisted grin on his lips. 'You know, she's got a powerful lot of stuff to pack up and move.'

Connor guffawed inanely. 'Shore 'nuff. Mayhaps, we can give her a hand.'

'If we were to ship her belongings off to Denver or Salt Lake,' Sandoval suggested, 'it would help to make up her mind. She can either follow after it or lose it!'

30

'That's a good idea,' his friend replied. ''Course, that there printing press will be hard to ship, being all big and awkward.'

Sandoval snapped his fingers. 'I know of a simple fix. We'll find us a hammer and break it into small pieces. That way we can fit the whole thing in a couple of burlap bags.'

'You bet,' Connor chortled. 'I'll go get—'

But the sound of horses approaching stopped the bruiser in mid-sentence. The pair rotated about to see two riders, the first of which was a bantam-sized fellow, decked out like a city dude, complete with a derby hat and a string tie dangling down in front. The other gent was more formidable looking, wearing regular travelling duds, leather gloves, and a flat-crowned Stetson. They stopped their horses a few feet shy of the walk.

'Lynette!' the dandy called to the woman. Then he swung a leg over the pommel and slid to the ground.

She returned the greeting, crying: 'Richard!' and ran over to him. The two of them hugged one another for a few moments.

'I got here quick as I could,' Richard told her, backing up from the heartfelt embrace.

'I've been worried about you coming all this way,' she reciprocated.

'Is this sissy your brother?' Sandoval scoffed, breaking into their reunion. 'Looks like a clown from a carnival, dressed in them frilly clothes.'

'Were you two accosting my sister?' Richard demanded in an exigent tone of voice. 'What do you want?'

'We've been suggesting she pack her trunk and head on down the road,' Sandoval stated harshly. 'If you want to keep all of your teeth, you'll help her to collect her gear and haul her carcass out of here pronto.'

Lynette informed him: 'This is Mr Sandoval and Mr Connor, the two men who attacked poor Tommy! He is only a boy, and they still kicked him when he was down. They nearly killed him.'

Richard squared off facing the two. 'How brave and daring of you men, viciously assaulting a defenceless youth.'

Sandoval took a menacing step forward. 'You squeak like a mouse, Mr Pansy-man. Maybe I ought to teach you about sticking your nose where it don't belong.'

Lynette observed the man who had arrived with Richard as he dismounted from his horse. An inch or two taller than most men, he had shoulders like a Greek god, and his facial features were masculine, and not altogether unattractive. He sported recently-barbered, sand-coloured hair and enigmatic, grey-blue eyes. He used the nearest hitch-rail to secure the reins of his mount, then moved nonchalantly over to stand next to her brother. He displayed an inoffensive countenance as he confronted the two lummoxes.

'We're not looking to provoke any disharmony, boys,' he said in a laid-back tone of voice. 'Richard only stopped by to visit his sister.'

'*Disharmony?*' Connor snorted contemptuously. 'What do that mean?'

Sandoval jeered: 'It means these two yahoos have come to help the ink-scribe shag her toys and whatever else she intends to take with her.' He puffed up his chest and took a step closer to the new arrival. 'We aim to see she leaves Deliverance ... and that means right this minute!'

The stranger continued to exhibit a tolerant mien. 'Come on, fella. My friend here hasn't seen his sister in several years. You can cut them a little slack.'

'We don't cut no one any slack, bucko.'

'The name is Mason.'

Sandoval gestured at Lynette and warned: 'If the woman and her printing press ain't gone in fifteen minutes, we're going to smash everything in her office to pieces!'

The change was subtle, but the muscles tightened along Mason's jaw and his flint-coloured eyes grew icy cold.

'I don't see you wearing badges, so you must have the backing of someone with authority or a lot of power hereabouts, huh?'

Connor stomped over to Sandoval's side. 'Look, Mr Nosy! We work for the mayor. We're peacekeepers here in town. That means no one does anything without our say-so.'

'Uh-huh.'

Sandoval thrust out his jaw and pointed at Mason's horse. 'That being said, you best hoist your butt up on that knock-kneed jackass of yours and ride back to wherever you came from.'

Lynette experienced a sting of keen disappointment as Mason's shoulders sagged and he began to turn. He was meekly going to do as he was told!

Abruptly, the man planted one foot and whirled back around. He struck hard and fast, driving a mighty fist into Sandoval's face. The force of the blow knocked him three steps backward before he lost his balance and landed flat on his back!

Lynette was dumbfounded by the sudden attack, but no more than Connor. Before he knew he was next in line for punishment, Mason turned on him. The man hastily tried to lift his fists in a protective posture, but a set of knuckles exploded against his jaw hard enough to rattle his teeth. Connor staggered uncertainly from the clout, both hands waving inanely to remain upright. The reflexive action proved futile. A second devastating punch sent him sprawling on the ground with his face digging a furrow in the dirt. Connor's body twitched slightly, but he was beyond rationale or the ability to get back up.

'I don't cotton to anyone insulting my horse, boys,' Mason announced to the two semi-conscious men. 'I'll expect an apology when your flyspeck brains are working again.'

As calmly as if he had shooed away a pesky hornet, Mason took a moment to present himself to Lynette, tipping his head slightly as he did so.

'Beg your pardon for the display of violence, Miss,' he apologized, touching his hat in a polite gesture. 'It isn't something a lady ought to have to witness.'

'Sis,' Richard cooed smugly, openly amused at her mouth being agape. 'This is Rod Mason, an associate of mine.'

As bold and confident as the man had been in dispatching the two tormentors, he appeared awkward and unsure of himself facing her.

'I'm pleased to meet you,' he said, unable to meet her inquiring gaze. 'Buster here has told me of your troubles. I'm right sorry about your hired man.'

'Thank you,' she managed, although her voice nearly squeaked. 'Tommy is the only one who dared to work for me. It cost him a severe beating.'

Mason looked past her to the doorway. 'Looks like a nice newspaper office.'

Lynette purposely moved a little so as to be directly in front of him. She critically eyed the two semi-conscious men.

'Who are you, Mr Mason? And why have you come to Deliverance?'

He locked gazes this time, consequent to her delivery expressing a measure of challenge. There was no hint of combativeness in his voice, however. He explained simply: 'Buster thought I might be of some assistance.'

She rotated her eyes to her brother once more. 'Rich?'

'Uh, well, you see, Sis. . . .' Richard paused, at a loss for an answer.

'Miss Brooks,' Mason politely rescued him from her inquisition. 'Could you tell me, is the mayor of Deliverance a fair-minded man?'

Lynette released Richard from her accusatory gaze and gave her head a negative shake. The action caused her long auburn locks to brush gently across her shoulders. 'No,' she replied firmly. 'The mayor is one of Harve Rutherford and Dealer Gilmore's cronies, and,' gesturing at the men Mason had subdued, 'this pair of offensive oafs work directly for the mayor, Mike Lafferty.'

'Mayor Lafferty,' he followed with another query, 'he appointed or elected to office?'

'He arrived as part of the gang who took over our town. He's a tyrant over the business owners as well as everyone who enters Deliverance.'

'With no official law in town, I don't suppose there is a jail?'

Lynette replied: 'Actually, there is.' She pointed up the street. 'That building standing alone was built to be a jail and sheriff's office, but there's never been a lawman since I moved here. The mayor uses the building as his office.'

'That's good news,' he said, pausing to ponder something in his mind. Then he reached down, grabbed Connor by the scruff of his neck and hoisted him up on his feet. Taking hold of the other man's shirt, he also dragged him upright. Both men swayed uncertainly, numbly testing their jaws and fingering the new bruises on their faces.

Lynette was about to inquire what he was going to do, when he suddenly asked: 'One last question.' She quickly offered a 'Yes?' and he ventured, 'Is there an honest person in town, one who most of the folks respect or admire?'

She considered the query and replied: 'I'd guess Doctor Wright is about the most well-thought-of person in town.'

'Thank you.' He touched the rim of his hat a second time in a polite gesture, then turned to Richard. 'I'll see you later,' he said. Then with a tilt of his head at the two dazed men, 'I need to square this little misunderstanding before it becomes a problem. I'd appreciate it if you would look after my horse.'

'Certainly,' Richard assured him. 'I'll be here with Lynette.'

Mason didn't speak again, but began herding the two bullies up the street towards the mayor's office.

Richard grinned when Lynette put a curious stare on him. 'Rich,' she murmured, perplexed by what had taken place, 'Tell me you didn't come here to start a war.'

'No, Sis,' he answered. 'But I came prepared to fight one if necessary.'

CHAPTER THREE

Mason stopped at the solidly-built structure. Where one would expect to see a sign reading Jail or Sheriff's Office, this one had a small shingle that read 'Mike Lafferty, City Mayor'.

He took a moment to remove the gun-belts and weapons off of his two captives and told them to sit on the porch. They did so without objection, other than moaning about the pain of their swollen faces. Mason entered through the office door to discover a thirty-ish, red-headed man, bulb nose, with bushy red brows and an untrimmed moustache, sitting behind a cluttered desk. On the paunchy side, the hombre looked like a cross between a hound dog and a red-hide buffalo with its winter coat.'Yeah?' he said, looking up from a *Farmer's Home Journal* magazine he'd been reading.

'Good afternoon . . . Mayor Lafferty?'

'That's right.'

Mason dumped the guns and holsters on his

desktop and paused to look around. His gaze lingered on the sturdy-looking twin jail cells at the rear of the building.

Allowing himself a satisfied grin, he returned his attention to the mayor.

'I see you have room for some prisoners. That's good.'

Lafferty canvassed the guns and belts on his desk, then scowled up at him. 'We do use this office for holding the occasional drunk or other lawbreaker. Kindly state your business.'

'First off, do you employ two men – names of Connor and Sandoval?'

'They work for this office – yes.'

'Meaning they take their orders from you?'

'If you're asking if I'm the one in charge of keeping order in Deliverance, Mr Nosy . . . the answer is also yes. What's this about?'

Mason slipped his gun out and pointed it at Lafferty. 'I'm placing you under arrest for extortion and for supporting harassment and assaults on the local citizenry.'

The blunt declaration and being at the muzzle-end of a gun caused Lafferty to rise up from his chair, eyes bugged and completely baffled.

'W-what are you talking about?' he stammered in wonder and confusion. 'Who are you?'

'Your exorbitant taxes are unwarranted and your two stumble-bum employees attacked the youth working for the town newspaper. Caught them red-handed harassing the lady editor. I'm told this isn't the first time you've turned your dogs loose on someone either. I reckon, by the time the circuit judge arrives, I'll have a few other witnesses and victims who will testify at your hearing.'

'My . . . my hearing?'

Before he could question the charges further, Mason waved his gun, motioning at the door. 'I've got your hired thugs on the porch. They both claim they were following your orders.'

'My orders! Wait a minute!' he wailed. 'The idea was to discourage the Brooks woman from writing slanderous trash about me and the other two leading citizens of our community. My men were only supposed to encourage her to be less critical. I gave no order about any rough stuff, least of all beating her young assistant.'

'We'll let a circuit judge sort out how much of the blame rests on your shoulders.'

'The quarrel has already been ruled upon,' he argued. 'Judge Barney took the case under advisement. It was deemed a minor physical altercation that got a little out of hand. He handed down a twenty dollar fine for each of my men.'

'I'm guessing a real judge might decide differently. I don't reckon your local magistrate is all that reliable or unbiased.'

'Who do you think you are?' Lafferty demanded to know. 'And on whose authority are you butting into the affairs of our town?'

'I'm a concerned citizen, and my authority is this here six-shooter,' Mason answered. 'Soon as you are locked away, I'll bring in your hired roughnecks to join you.'

'But I'm the mayor of Deliverance! You can't treat me like an ordinary criminal.'

Mason deliberately cocked back the hammer on his Colt. 'Say what?'

'Uh,' Lafferty paled, staring at the gun. 'I mean, you have no case against me.'

'Where are the keys to the cells?'

The mayor's gun and belt were hanging on a hook next to his suit-coat and hat. He tipped his head in that direction so Mason would see a keyring and set of keys.

Mason retrieved the ring and prodded Lafferty with the muzzle of his gun, directing him to the first cell. He patted him down to check for any concealed weapons before he closed the door and turned the key in the lock. Shortly thereafter, his two employees were secured in the adjacent cell. Both Sandoval and Connor were clamouring for water and complaining about their aching heads. He gave them what water was in the office and left the three of them to their miseries.

Stopping at the entrance, he found the key for the front door. Pausing to remove the mayor's shingle, he tossed it inside the office, then locked the place up and took the keys with him. He figured, even if someone heard the prisoners yelling, they wouldn't be able to get in and let the trio loose for a bit. Besides which, he didn't intend to be gone for very long.

A short search located the sign of J. Wright, MD. It was tacked to the front of a small house a short way along the main street of town, well cared for, including a tidy bed of flowers along its short pathway to the front door. He observed there was room for a wagon or a couple horses next to the structure, with a row of houses and shops to either side.

A tiny bell, dangling from a hook above the door, announced his arrival when Mason stepped through the entrance way. He discovered the interior was an office of sorts, with a long, cushioned exam table, adequate for a patient to sit or lie down upon. There were cupboards and a wash basin, along with numerous bottles of potions and pills along a shelf. To the rear were the living quarters. He stopped before proceeding further and removed his hat.

Momentarily, a grey-haired lady stepped out of the adjacent room to meet him. Short, not more than five foot in height, she was matronly in build, but had steady green eyes. Both strength and compassion were imbedded in her facial features.

She smiled a greeting. 'You look about as healthy as a two-year-old bull,' were her words of welcome. 'What can I do for you?'

Mason twisted his hat in his hands, uncomfortable around the fairer sex, regardless of their age. 'I'm here to see the doc.'

'That would be me,' she replied professionally. 'John, my husband, was a doctor for twenty-odd years. I started out as his nurse or aide and took over the practice when he died. I left the "J" on the sign out front because my first name is Julia.'

'Miss Brooks said you were about the most respected person in town.'

She laughed at the statement. 'No one dares bad-mouth the only doctor for a hundred miles around, sonny. Could be, they might need me to save their life or limb one day.'

Her humour put him more at ease. 'Well, I've a mind to put a stop to the tax fraud, intimidation, and downright abuse of the citizens and decent folks hereabouts.'

The woman re-evaluated him with a cool scrutiny. 'Did you bring along the army?'

'No, ma'am. That's why I'm here to see you.'

'I was down the street, doing some shopping, a few minutes ago. I happened to see you . . .' she searched for the definition she wanted, 'introduce yourself to Connor and Sandoval. I rather expected one or both of them to come by asking for treatment.' She gave him a critical evaluation. 'Never seen two grown men taken down any quicker than you did that pair of coyotes – one or two punches each!' She scrutinized his muscular frame. 'Close up, you look about as capable as any man I ever met.'

'Those fellows are trying to run Miss Brooks out of the valley.' He shrugged. 'They seemed to think they could run me off too – insulted my horse in the process. Well,' he stated manifestly, 'I don't allow no-accounts to make fun of my dependable steed.'

She laughed at his explanation. 'And the mayor? What did he have to say about you manhandling his two hired grunts?'

'Didn't come up,' Mason told her. 'He was busy cussing at me for locking him in one of his own cells. I've got all three of them varmints stowed away at the sheriff's office.'

'You mean the mayor's office.'

'It's not his office any more.'

The news caused the woman's eyes to widen in

surprise. 'So you arrested Mayor Lafferty?'

'Seemed the best way to start this here project. This town needs a fair and impartial justice system. I've been told the mayor is part of the problem. His men also attempted to silence the press, the result of which ended with a young man being nearly killed a short while back.'

'Tommy Smith,' she acknowledged. With a curious glint in her eyes, she said: 'You sound well educated in the field of law.'

'I've been on both sides of a jail cell the past few years,' he explained. 'Plus, I've just finished several days with Miss Brooks' brother. He outlined the problems of this town until I was sick of listening to him talk.'

The statement caused Julia to smile. 'I see.'

'Like I told you, I need an ally, and Miss Brooks said you were respected around town.'

'Explain what you want of me, young man,' Julia proceeded cautiously. 'Then I'll decide if I can help you or not.'

Julia walked over to Will Barney's house. It was little more than a shack, but the judge liked to think of himself as a successful magistrate. He had a woman living with him – supposedly his spinster sister-in-law, but most around town knew she was a live-in cook, housekeeper and companion.

The woman answered the door in a ragged housecoat. When Julia related why she had come, the gal yelled over her shoulder: 'Someone to see you, Willy!' Then she left Julia standing at the entrance and wandered off to the back of the two-room abode.

Judge Barney was in his fifties, unshaven for several days, with a nearly bald head and the red-rimmed eyes of a hard drinker. Built like a pot-belly stove, he had large ears that stood out from his head like a stagecoach with both doors open.

'Julia, my dear!' he greeted her blandly. 'What brings you to my doorstep?'

She disliked the fact that, sporting the title of a judge, Barney felt his status allowed him to call everyone by their first name. Hiding the sensation, she offered up a smile.

'We've a little excitement I thought you should know about.'

'Excitement? In our fair town?'

'The mayor and his two hired rowdies are behind bars – charged with assaulting Tommy Smith and verbally threatening Miss Brooks.'

Barney blinked and his face twisted in shock. 'What?' he croaked hoarsely. 'Who put them behind bars?'

'A rather competent fellow by the name of Rod Mason. He arrested the three of them and has been proclaimed sheriff . . . by order of the interim mayor.'

'Interim mayor?' Barney floundered in confusion. 'Who appointed an interim mayor?'

'Mr Mason, the man who is now sheriff.'

Barney slapped his brow, even more befuddled. 'Hold on!' he said, trying to make sense of what Julia was telling him. 'A sheriff can be appointed by an acting mayor, but I never heard of a non-elective sheriff selecting his own mayor!' He puffed up his chest and ire

45

caused a red flush in his cheeks. 'If anyone has the authority to do any appointing, it would be me!'

'I'm here as a courtesy,' Julia went on calmly, ignoring his outburst. 'I wanted you to be aware of what had happened.'

The man's eyes remained bulging at the bizarre tidings, but finally rasped out the question: 'Who, may I ask, is this new interim mayor?'

'That would be me.'

Barney's face increased to a darker shade of red. 'You mean to tell me that you appointed the sheriff, after he appointed you?'

'Yes, it happened something like that.' Julia clarified the chain of events: 'He suggested I assume the position of mayor, as Mike Lafferty is likely to be sent to prison. Once I accepted the job, I took it upon myself to appoint him sheriff.'

The judge was reeling, trying to decide if the doctor had gone totally mad, or if his own mind had suddenly taken a journey down a burrow of utter nonsense. He sputtered and mumbled for a few seconds, then turned to get his hat and coat.

'I'd better have a talk with this man, Julia. None of these actions can be sanctioned without the approval of the reigning authority in Deliverance. I'm the judge. Therefore, I am the one who will decide who can or can't be appointed to what position.'

'Mr Mason thought you might see it that way,' Julia responded.

The man came out of the house, shoving his arms into the sleeves of his worn, black suit-coat. He also donned a black top hat that had lost much of its blocking, and started up the street, taking long, determined strides. Julia had to hurry to keep up with him as they marched to the mayor's office and through the front door.

Mason was sitting behind what had been the mayor's desk, sorting through handbills and wanted notices he'd found shoved in the bottom drawer. He ignored Barney's arrival, but rose to his feet when Julia entered the office a couple steps behind him.

'Mayor Wright,' he greeted her cordially. 'Good to see you again.'

'What's all this hogwash, young man?' Barney bellowed. 'I personally heard the case concerning Tommy Smith. The court deemed his beating was the result of an insignificant altercation.'

'This the would-be magistrate?' Mason asked Julia. At her nod, he put a hard look on the judge.

'I find no official document here that allows you are any kind of judge,' he stated. 'When and where did you receive your appointment?'

Barney made a face. 'Mayor Lafferty designated me the town judge. It was one of his first duties of his office. I was a lawyer for several years, so I know the law.'

'So do I, Barney,' Mason replied. 'As Mr Lafferty was never an official mayor, he had no authority to appoint anyone to such a lofty post.'

'Lafferty was named mayor by the townspeople!' Barney argued.

'You have a town council?'

'Well, no, but it was a unanimous decision by the most prominent citizens in town.'

'That so?' Mason looked to Julia. 'Were you invited?'

'No,' she answered. 'This all came about when Mr Rutherford and his men arrived in town and took over the bank and saloon a few months back. Since that time, they have ruled over the entire town. Up until their arrival, we had an open session in place for the citizens whenever there was a problem to be solved.'

Barney glared at the doctor. 'You're twisting this askew; putting everything in a bad light, Julia!'

'You don't want to insinuate the mayor is telling falsehoods in front of me, Barney,' Mason warned. 'Not unless you want a busted nose and a jail cell for defaming her character.'

The ex-judge took a step back and the blood drained from his face. 'Well . . . I meant no offence,' he muttered. 'This is all so sudden. I don't—'

'We have wired for a circuit judge,' Mason cut him off. 'If you'd care to offer a transcript from your hearing concerning the assault on Tommy Smith, it would be appreciated.'

'Transcript?' he mumbled.

'You keep a record of all court proceedings, do you not?'

Barney shuffled his feet. 'Uh, not exactly.'

'Then we will hold court without your input,' Mason announced. 'Until we get things sorted out, there won't be any need for a falsely-appointed judge. One will be elected or appointed once the tax fraud, bullying and land grabbing is cleared up. Feel free to submit your name when time for the nomination arrives.'

The man's shoulders sagged and he shook his head.

Without the position of judge, there would be no monthly payment from Rutherford and Gilmore. Will Barney was suddenly a beaten man, wondering where he could find a job that would keep him fed and housed . . . and catered to by Verona, his housekeeper. He sullenly backed out the door and shuffled off down the street.

Julia watched him go and cocked her head to speak over her shoulder. 'Soon as he is over the shock, he'll spread the word of what's happened. Once Harve Rutherford is informed of the goings-on, your life is going to become a lot more complicated, and probably much shorter.'

'Reckon I've started something of an avalanche.'

Julia bobbed her head in agreement. 'I hope we don't both get buried alive when it hits.'

The town runner handed Richard the message. In return, a nickle from his pocket put a smile on the boy's face. Soon as he left, Lynette looked over Richard's shoulder so she could read the note.

'Dear Lord!' she gasped. 'Richard! What have you done?'

Her brother laughed. 'Didn't I tell you? Mason is a man of action.'

'Action?' she cried. 'He'll be dead before nightfall. How can he assume the position of sheriff and install a new mayor? Who does he think he is?'

'He wants me to help watch the jail,' Richard evaded an answer. 'I better get my shotgun and head over and see him.'

49

'It's getting late and you need to eat supper,' Lynette countered. 'We'll take Mr Mason a meal too. I don't care what he feeds the prisoners, but he's risking his life to help me and the townsfolk. I won't have him eating a can of beans or a dry crust of bread for his meals.'

'Good idea. It will show him you are not only smart, but you're a good cook too.'

'Richard,' Lynette spoke softly. 'Are you sure this man can handle such a major task? I mean, Rutherford's bunch has a lot of money and guns. How can one man take on an army?'

'You saw him in action, Sis. He flattened those two bullies without breaking a sweat. They don't call him Lightning Rod Mason for nothing. He strikes fast and hard.'

'Yes, but taking on a half-dozen men at one time . . .'

'He'll come up with a plan, Sis. You wait and see.'

Lynette regarded him with a forlorn look. 'I hope you and your capable friend haven't come all this way to end up residents in the local cemetery.'

Rutherford and Dealer were sitting down at the supper table. They shared the house, with a hired cook and housekeeper to tend to their every whim. The plate of roast beef and potatoes was in the middle of the table when Baron Kent entered the room. He was a man who dressed in black, sported a pair of twin Colts with burnished walnut handles, and boots that never lacked for polish. His spurs were genuine silver and jingled with each step. Vain about his appearance, Baron walked the path of a hired gun, as deadly as any man in the country.

He drew top wages and was something of a foreman, tending to duties concerning security for the bank as well as the saloon. He was one of three who had joined up with Rutherford and Dealer when they formed a gang in Texas. The other two were Scraps – a brawl-loving brute – and Mike Lafferty.

'You eat yet?' Rutherford asked him. 'The cook can bring another plate.'

Baron waved a hand. 'No thanks, Harve. I grabbed a bite earlier.'

'You hear the news?' Dealer wanted to know.

Baron grinned. 'Yeah, the judge cornered me at the saloon. He's worried sick about losing his cushy job.'

'Did you get a look at this guy, this Mason character?' Rutherford wanted to know. 'Where does he get off taking over our town?'

'Dunno, but he arrived with the newswoman's brother. He has wired for a circuit judge – should be here in a coupla weeks. That's when Doctor Wright says there will be an election for mayor and sheriff.'

'What about Lafferty and his two flunkies?'

'There will be a hearing concerning Tommy Smith's beating and the misuse of tax monies. As for the rest of us, evidence will be given about how you've raised interest rates and forced some of the farmers and businesses out.'

'Banks set their own interest rates all over the country,' Rutherford dismissed the news. 'I'm not worried about what a judge might find.'

'Yes, but the intimidation, the beatings ... the banker's disappearance?' Baron shook his head. 'There

51

might be cause for an investigation.'

'If that don't beat all!' Dealer joined in the conversation. 'Where did this guy come from and how did he cause so much trouble in such a short period of time?'

'We can't let him take over as sheriff,' Rutherford said. 'We need to keep control of things.'

'Might get some support around town concerning the judge, but not the mayor,' Baron pointed out. 'Lafferty came with us as an outsider. Add to that, he's been in charge of collecting taxes and fees from the businessmen, yet he hasn't made any improvements for the town.'

Dealer sighed in agreement. 'Add the fact his two rock-head enforcers have ran roughshod over everyone in town. No one is going to vote for him, not without a gun to their head.'

'If Lafferty and his boys end up on trial, one of them will sure enough point a finger at us,' Baron warned. 'We'll be lucky to keep from ending up in jail with them.'

Rutherford pondered their situation. 'Julia isn't going to buck the odds; she's too smart for that. We only have to deal with this lone wolf. We need to cut him down to size and run him out of town.'

'You thinking of Scraps?' Baron queried.

Rutherford gave his head a nod. 'Break a few of this honcho's bones, gouge out an eye – Scraps' specialty – and he'll leave with his tail dragging.'

Dealer asked: 'Want to send him over tonight?'

'Tomorrow is soon enough. Tell him to get a good night's sleep so he is well rested. He'll want to do a thorough job on this high-minded joker.'

'You know, I could deal with this in a more permanent fashion,' Baron bragged.

'Killing the man wouldn't look good to a travelling judge. We'll give this interloper a push. If that ain't enough . . .' Rutherford let the words hang, then added with finality, '. . . you can put his name on a rock.'

CHAPTER FOUR

Mason felt an expectant surge, something warm infusing the blood running through his veins, at seeing Lynette again. She was accompanying Richard to the newly converted sheriff's office. He took note that she was wearing a flattering yellow dress, with white lace about the neckline and sleeves. Her freshly-combed hair brushed her shoulders as she walked, looking as soft and delicate as fine strains of silk. The auburn colour glinted like autumn-leaf gold in the setting sunlight, and her complexion equalled that of an ivory statue. He stood in the open door to greet them, and held it so Richard could enter past him with a tray and three plates of food. Lynette's brother continued inside to feed the prisoners, while she halted at the step and placed a basket down on the porch.

'Richard and I already ate,' she informed him, her voice soft and oddly hesitant. 'I'll keep you company, if that's all right?'

'I'd be honoured, Miss Brooks,' Mason said quickly, sitting down. Lynette had prepared a complete meal, with a plate, napkin, and a pint of lemonade. She put down a cloth to sit on, preventing her dress from touching the dusty porch. Then she removed items of food, served up his meal and he began to eat.

The conversation was cordial, with no mention of the prisoners inside the newly designated sheriff's office. He found the young lady uncertain and reserved, as if she wasn't comfortable around a strange man. It was queerly gratifying, because he also suffered from being awkward and ambivalent of himself around her. He finally summoned his courage to breech the ungainly bridge between them.

'I admit to not having much practice when it comes to talking to a pretty, educated gal,' he confessed. 'But I surely don't mean to frighten you.'

'Frighten me?'

'Yeah, well I come charging in like a bull after a couple stray coyotes didn't I? Busted those two fellers a good one each before I even said "howdy" to you.'

'You were acting on my behalf,' she excused the violent introduction. 'Men like Sandoval and Connor don't respect any normal form of reasoning, only brute force.'

'Them I know how to handle,' he said. 'I can deal with the worst most men can throw at me, but I'm plum backward around a lady such as yourself. I don't know how to behave.'

Lynette surprised him with a timorous smile. 'It isn't only you, Mr Mason. I . . . I had a rather bad experience with a man, a philanderer who took advantage of my naivety and lack of experience around men. I was hurt and mortified by the episode and have discouraged suitors ever since.'

'I'm not familiar with what one of them philanderer-types does for a living.'

'It isn't an occupation, it means he was a womanizing, underhanded scoundrel.'

Mason frowned. 'Tell me his name and where I can find him, Miss. I'll settle for your honour and the lowly hunk of vermin will crawl all the way back here on his hands and knees to apologize.'

She laughed at his threat, the mirth signalling a lowering of her guard. 'I actually believe you.'

'Honesty is one of my few virtues,' he admitted.

Lynette shifted subjects. 'Richard told me you have a brother.'

'Yeah, Cliff is five years younger than me. He works for our uncles.'

'Uncles?'

'Three brothers – the Valerons. They have a sizable place on the Colorado-Wyoming border. Ma's sister is married to one of the three. Got more cousins than I can count in that big family.'

'But you choose to be . . . what? A troubleshooter of some kind?'

'No, ma'am. I'm more of a wanderer – a tumbleweed driven before the wind.'

'How did Richard and you become friends?'

He grinned at her query, enjoying the middling conversation. His candid gaze caused her features to soften noticeably and he was completely disarmed. Lynette was quite fetching when her guard was down. She afforded a feminine 'ahem' to prompt him to recover his power of speech.

'Uh, sorry,' Mason said, embarrassed to have lost his train of thought. 'You were asking about buster and me?'

'Yes, you seem . . . well, you're not exactly the kind of man Richard usually pals around with.'

'Not as book-learned, you mean?'

She laughed again, once more affecting him with her natural charm. 'That's it exactly. Richard's friends are mostly bank colleges or businessmen.'

'Actually, he paid my fine to get me out of jail.'

The remark caused her to gape. She recouped her senses to inquire: 'He did what?'

'Yes, ma'am. I was sitting out a ten-day sentence for settling a dispute between a couple hunters and an Indian scout. A fight broke out during a town barbecue and I reckon them two would have killed the Indian, if I hadn't taken up for him.'

'Yet, they put you in jail?'

'Indians aren't real popular in this part of the country. Nearly every person you meet has lost a friend or loved one to a hostile band.' He shrugged. 'Difference is, this red man was working for the army as a scout; he was on our side.'

'So why did the judge incarcerate you?'

'Our little fracas intruded on his dinner party.' At her inquisitive look, he explained. 'I knocked one of the men over the table where he and his wife were sitting. They both ended up wearing a fair portion of their meal.'

The corners of her mouth rose slightly at the image,

but she remained serious. 'So, do you enjoy physical conflicts?'

'Not at all,' he defended. 'I figure there has to be order in our society. Men shouldn't be browbeaten or pushed around just because they're different or nature chose to make them slighter in build. Plus, I don't much like bullies.'

'And that's why you learned how to fight.' It was a statement of fact. When Mason had nothing more to say, Lynette continued.

'Richard explained to me about your training.' She uttered a girlish giggle. 'And how utterly hopeless he was as your student.'

Mason's grinned at the memory. 'If a man wanted someone to plan his finances or check a storekeeper's books, your brother would be the man for the job. When it comes to fighting, his best option is to use what little speed God gave him and run for the hills.'

Lynette smiled at his summation, but turned serious. 'I believe you are capable, Mr Mason, but I don't see how one man can go up against Rutherford and Gilmore. Those two have some dangerous men working for them.'

'Tell me about the opposition.'

'Five of them arrived here from Texas, packing a lot of money and guns. Within a week, they took control of the bank and the saloon. Most of the land and businesses around here were already in debt, as the bank held their deeds. Rutherford increased the interest rate until a few people went broke. That allowed him to resell those properties and make a tidy profit.'

'And they get away doing that, because there is no law

hereabouts to deal with them,' Mason deduced.

'Mike Lafferty assumed the position of mayor and they also hired their own judge. You've already introduced yourself to Lafferty's men. Between them and Rutherford, they have control over the entire valley.'

'We kind of fired the judge, me and Mrs Wright.'

Lynette shook her head in wonder. 'Dear me, you do work quickly.'

'I aim to put an end to them fellows' stranglehold. If it becomes more than I can handle alone, I'll send for a couple of my cousins. When it comes to good men, the Valerons have a code of honour that few families can match. Like them, I believe that whenever or wherever crime or corruption is unchecked, it is a slap to every honest citizen's face. I'm one of them citizens who slap right back!'

Lynette reached out and placed her hand on his arm. 'I realize you are sincere, Mr Mason, but I don't want to see you hurt or killed.'

'It's not like I'd be missed all that much,' he said rather flippantly.

The woman frowned. 'Don't you dare say that!' she snapped. 'Men of courage and laurels are always needed. You are risking your life for people you don't even know. I've never met anyone who would do that before.'

'Well, buster is a friend.'

'He is a stranger,' her voice rose with her passion, 'who bailed you out of jail and hired you to come here. I'm sure he didn't expect you would attempt to tame the entire valley alone!'

'Not so loud,' he shushed her placidly. 'The whole

town will hear you.'

Lynette didn't have to reply or react, as Richard appeared at the doorway, carrying the three empty dishes.

'Them fellows cleaned the last breadcrumb from their plates, Sis,' he announced. 'It's like I always told you – you're a mighty fine cook.'

'I agree completely, Miss Brooks,' Mason praised, rising quickly to his feet. He reached down to take hold of the lady's wrist and helped her to stand. 'I haven't had such fine cooking since I left home.'

'You're more than welcome,' Lynette said stiffly, likely worried Richard had overheard her outburst. To cover her chagrin, she picked up her basket and the piece of protective cloth, which she stuck in the container. Composed once more, she paused to regard Mason with a look of genuine concern. 'Do be careful. These are dangerous men and are not to be taken lightly. They won't sit by and let you wrestle the town free from their control.'

Mason grunted. 'No town should be terrorized by a band of hard-cases with guns. People have the right to govern themselves.'

'I'll be around if you need me,' Richard offered. 'I left my shotgun at Lynette's office, but I can get it quick enough.'

'You take tonight off, buster,' Mason offered. 'You can help watch the jail tomorrow.'

He said 'OK' and Lynette lifted her free hand in a short wave. Then they returned down the street towards the newspaper office and Lynette's upstairs apartment.

Mason watched them go and felt a renewed tug at his heart strings. It didn't take a lot of contemplation to realize he was missing out on the best thing in life . . . a wife and family of his own.

After a restless night on a cot, which he bought at the general store, Mason arose to the grumblings of his three incarcerated guests. He addressed them with a succinct – 'Shut up or you can chew your own boot leather for breakfast!' – and there was tranquility in the jail once more.

Julia arranged for the prisoners' meals to be prepared at the Harmony House eating establishment, and also provided that Mason would eat for free. Mike Lafferty had a tax structure in place, so there were funds available to pay for everything in due process.

As Mason had been privileged to dine with Lynette the previous night, he didn't bother ordering anything special for breakfast. Mush and toast was good enough for the men he was holding, so he got himself the same. Crossing the street to his office with the tray of food, he spotted a lone rider. The man's girth was equal to his mount and he looked out of place on the back of a horse. Mason didn't pay him any attention outwardly, but he kept an eye on him while entering the jail.

Once he served the three inmates, he mentioned to Lafferty: 'A walking outhouse rode in on a dun horse. He's wearing a lot of rawhide, including knee-high moccasin boots. His ten-gallon hat looked like something he stole from a scarecrow.'

The ex-mayor grinned. 'He has a shanty outside of

town. Goes by the name of Scraps, 'cause that's all he leaves behind when he tears a man to pieces.'

'He claims to have gouged an eye out of six different men,' Sandoval spoke up.

'Scraps is here for your hide, Mason,' Connor warned. 'You ought to light a'shuck before he tracks you down!'

Mason responded evenly. 'Given a choice, I'm more apt to fight than run. I'll be sure and give Scraps a chance to make the same decision.'

'He'll eat you alive!' Connor jeered.

'Carve your heart out with his skinning knife,' mouthed Sandoval.

As for Lafferty, he just kept right on grinning.

Rather than reply to the taunting, Mason removed the special thick-hide gloves he carried in his belt and stepped out the door.

Scraps had a face that would have made potential mothers swear off parenthood – piggish eyes above a wide, crooked nose, with several gaping holes in his row of tobacco-stained teeth. With a horseshoe-shaped jaw and a scraggly, unshaven face, he would have been plug-ugly without the lengthy, greasy hair that hung to his shoulders. Blocky in build, his ape-like arms were covered with coarse hair and as big around as Mason's thighs.

'I come to rip you apart like a toy doll,' Scraps announced, skipping any introduction. 'You can run if you don't have the sand for a beating.'

'Never cottoned to bullies who destroyed children's toys,' Mason riposted. 'And I'm not exactly intimidated by a man whose nickname is taken from odds and ends.'

The brute's thick lips parted in a sneer, the same look one might expect from a rabid wolverine. 'You've a funny mouth, mister. I think I'll shut it . . . permanently.'

Mason doubled his fists within the thick-lined gloves and primed himself for combat. Never one to allow anger to dictate his game, he methodically sized up his opponent: Bull. Bear. Mauling dog. Scraps would use his size and muscle to dominate the fight. If he got hold of Mason, he could do the most damage using his superior strength. Mason had met men in the ring like him before. None more formidable than the giant before him, but he had honed his skill and was a seasoned veteran. He silently prayed the speed and power behind his punches would give him the advantage.

Scraps went from standing to a charge without shifting his stance. A less prepared fighter might have been caught flat-footed at the suddenness of the attack.

However, Mason reacted swiftly. He sidestepped the rush and, simultaneously, launched a left jab that nailed the man squarely on the nose. Before Scraps could alter his speed or direction, Mason whirled in behind him and slammed him hard to the back of his left ear. The power of which drove him to his knees.

Scraps was game and quick for a man of his size. He scrambled to his feet instantly and spun about to face Mason. Throwing up a defensive posture to protect his face, he blinked at the tears to clear his vision from the poke in the nose. Before he could set himself, Mason leapt forward and slipped a second jab between the man's knotted fists, cracking him hard on the bridge of the nose once more.

Mason repeated the strategy, staying out of the man's reach, then darting in close enough to use his left jab to blind the big oaf again and again. When Scraps was forced to lift his guard up in front of his face, Mason launched a solid right-left combination to hammer his opponent in the stomach and kidneys. This time his adversary grunted from the power behind the blows.

Moving constantly, Mason remained patient, avoiding every omnipotent attempt the muscular brute made to hit or ensnare him within his grasp. In and out, back and forth, he continued to pulverize his opponent with wicked punches to the body and head.

Scraps began to gasp for breath, weary of chasing after the artful boxer, and feeling the effects of a thorough beating. He grew desperate, knowing he only had to get his hands on the elusive fighter, then he would break his foe in half and crush him under his heels.

But Mason was nowhere and everywhere at the same time. The direful jabs continually smashed his broken nose and caused an infernal swelling about his eyes. Staggering blindly, Scraps had yet to land a single blow. Every charge ended with him on his belly in the dust, every swing of his fists got nothing but air. His lungs were afire from the effort exerted, but pausing to pant for air allowed his adversary to pummel him with rock-hard contact to the body that felt like each blow was delivered by an eight-pound hammer. Subsequently, Scraps' energy waned and both eyes were closed to mere slits from swelling. That's when a bone-shattering punch exploded against his jaw. The force was great enough to lift him up on to his toes. Dazed, the world went dark. A moment later, there was the taste of dirt and blood in his mouth.

'Might want to stay down, tough guy,' a controlled voice reached his semi-conscious brain. 'You'll not be gouging out any eyes today.'

Scraps was vaguely aware of a set of strong arms half-dragging and half-carrying him. After he managed a few staggering steps, he landed on a solid wooden floor. Even as he struggled to reach a level of awareness, Mike Lafferty's voice echoed in his ears.

'Damn, Scraps! I thought you were supposed to be tough!'

CHAPTER FIVE

Wyatt Valeron was at the main ranch house, preparing for an extended hunt with Jared. Beef, pork and mutton were staples on the ranch, but everyone liked venison and buffalo meat as well. The two cousins had planned a trip to the Dakotas to hunt deer and elk. There were still some herds of buffalo around, but they no longer shook the earth when they began to run. Their numbers had dwindled from countless millions to only a few thousand, their way of life gone via the westward expansion of America's populace.

Cliff Mason, a cousin who had become part of the family, was in the yard watching Nessy, a rescued orphan who had adopted him as her father. She was laughing and playing a game of 'tag' with two other children – kids of some Valeron employees – when a rider entered the yard.

'It's Skip,' Wyatt informed Jared, speaking of the store manager/telegraph operator in town. 'Don't see him on a horse very often.'

'Must be important for him to ride out here instead of

sending a runner from town.'

Locke Valeron, the senior member of the family and acknowledged ramrod of the vast Valeron holdings, had been working in his den with Martin, his nephew and the ranch accountant. He overheard their conversation and rambled out to stand alongside his son, Jared. He was the one to greet their friend and employee from town.

Cliff left Nessy with the other children and wandered over to join the group.

'Trouble,' was the single word Skip offered, handing a piece of paper to Locke.

'It's your brother,' Locke spoke to Cliff as he read the note. 'He got himself shot in the back over at Deliverance.'

'Mason?' Cliff asked, dismayed at the news. 'Is he . . .?'

'Says he is being looked after by some folks he was helping.'

'Blast his hide!' Cliff cried. 'Last I heard, he was in Denver. Bet he's mixed up in someone else's problems.'

Locke looked up from the paper. 'This here is from the mayor, a gent named J. Wright. He said Mason was trying to help the town's newspaper editor and was shot for his efforts. He's asking we send help at once.'

'Didn't I tell you?' Cliff wailed. 'He's always sticking his nose where it don't belong!'

'So much for our hunting trip,' Wyatt said, addressing the request. 'Jared and I will go have a look-see.'

'I'm going too!' Cliff exclaimed. 'He's my brother!'

Locke gave a shake of his head. 'That little orphan girl needs you more than your brother. We've got a dozen men who can ride to Deliverance, but only you can take care of her.'

'By Hannah! This is completely unfair.'

Locke pointed out, 'Everyone in her life has been taken from her, even the nun who was transporting her to an orphan home. You can't leave her while she's so dependent on you.'

'She likes Aunt Faye, Tish and Wendy,' Cliff argued. 'One of them could watch over her for a few days.'

'Wendy is in Denver, shopping with her mother and Aunt Gwen,' Wyatt pointed out. 'And my mother has too many chores with them gone to worry about Nessy.'

'That still leaves Tish,' Cliff said.

Jared snickered at the notion. 'Tish doesn't do anyone any favours, if there isn't something in it for her. You'd have a better chance trading a blind horse to Shane.'

'Yeah, but—'

'I'll go in Cliff's place,' a bass voice spoke up from a short way off. As the men turned to see the speaker, Landau Queen approached the group. He had been close by, harnessing a horse to a carriage for Scarlet Valeron, who was going to town to pick up the weekly groceries with her younger sister. 'I'm a fair hand in a fight,' he stated, 'and I owe you folks a debt.'

Locke's features modulated when he faced the man. 'You protected and looked after Scarlet when she was kidnapped, son. You've nothing to prove.'

'Kilt the man who took her!' Jared supported his father's comment. Then with a wry grin, 'Beat me to it. Guess you do owe me something for that.'

'I was riding with the men who took your daughter . . . all the way to Brimstone.' Landau shook his head. 'I should have never let that happen.'

'No one would expect a lone man to stand up to five ruthless outlaws,' Wyatt allowed. 'You did what you could to ensure her safety. That's why you're now working for us.'

Landau didn't back down. 'All the same, I'd be right proud to ride with the boys.'

Jared chuckled. 'You don't fool me. You figure to win us over so you can court my sister with our blessing.'

The man didn't argue; he simply smiled.

'All right,' Locke made the decision. 'The three of you grab your gear and head for Deliverance. If you need help, you only have to send word. Reese can get a dozen men and even toss his Gatling gun in a wagon if need be.'

'I still ought to be going,' Cliff grumbled.

'You can't go without taking Nessy, and we don't want her being in danger,' Wyatt argued. 'No one much cares if you get yourself shot up or killed, but that little girl deserves a chance at a real life.'

Cliff shook his head and grumbled. 'Don't know why I ever come here. All I get for my efforts is picked on and treated like a stray dog.'

'A stray dog we put up with,' Jared quipped, 'so long as you keep Nessy happy.'

He harrumphed. 'Having a way with females – it sure come round to bite me on the rump!'

Mason fought to break surface through the black void. Finally, he forced a crack in one eyelid and reached full consciousness. He discovered he was lying in bed, with a feather pillow under his head. Sunlight shone through a single window, adorned with pink curtains, trimmed with white lace. Obviously, this was not a man's bedroom.

'Are you back with us?' a soft voice asked at his side.

Mason lacked the strength to turn his head. He searched for enough moisture to form a word. 'W-water?'

After a moment and some shuffling of feet, Lynette's face appeared above him. Her hand slid under the back of his neck and she lifted his head forward. The tipped cup of water pressed against his lips and he was able to slake the dryness in his throat. She pulled the cup away once he'd finished drinking and appeared to study him with a critical eye.

'Julia didn't think you'd wake up today. She spent a full thirty minutes removing that bullet from your back.'

'I don't remember much of anything.'

'How about your battle with Scraps?'

'Yeah, I recall tossing him in the cell with the ex-mayor.'

'Well, you were making a round through town about dark and someone shot you from behind. No one saw who pulled the trigger, but it looked as if you might die from the wound.'

'You predicted I'd get myself shot.'

'Julia was afraid the gunman would come to finish the job if you stayed at her place. Richard helped us carry you up to my apartment after she removed the bullet. She told everyone you had died and even had the carpenter fashion a coffin. Richard added to the ruse by hiring a couple of men to dig a grave.'

'Hope you don't expect me to climb in a box and get buried alive.'

'No, we are going to put a couple sacks of grain in the casket and have the funeral this afternoon. That way, no one will be looking for you.'

Mason sighed. 'Greenhorn mistake, allowing someone to shoot me.' He added: 'Bigger mistake, them not getting the job done.'

'Julia sent a wire to your relatives – the Valerons.'

'Reckon I'll have some help right sudden. That side of the family takes it real personal when someone tries to kill one of their kin.'

'Do you think you could eat something?'

'Don't want to put you to any trouble, Miss Brooks.'

She clicked her tongue. 'What kind of thing is that to say! You get yourself shot while trying to protect my newspaper and make this a decent town to live in, and I'm not supposed to take care of you?'

Mason swallowed hard. 'I . . . well, I've never been looked after by a proper lady. I don't know the rules.'

'Regardless of the situation, the rules are always the same, Mr Mason. When a woman offers her service, you either chose to graciously accept – or find yourself in a world of trouble if you decline!'

He managed a crooked grin at the impassioned words. 'Seems the wiser choice to accept.'

'Wiser in all sorts of ways,' she concurred bluntly.

Before she could exit the room, he asked: 'Them there situations? Does that encompass everything?'

'Everything?'

'I'm a might curious . . . about romance?' he wondered aloud. 'Do the same set of rules hold true for that too?'

'It's a trifle early in our relationship to ask such a question,' she reciprocated.

'Well, I'm already in your bedroom. That ought to count for something.'

Lynette used a scolding tone of voice to reply. 'I see you were telling the truth, claiming to have never been looked after by a proper lady.'

'Right. My mistake,' he apologized. 'I'm beholding to you for seeing to my care.'

'Besides,' her voice muted slightly, 'I told you before, I haven't been courted in some time. As for actual love, I believe that is a luxury many people can never afford. There are too many needs to be met in life, goals to be achieved.'

'Pardon my saying so, Miss Brooks, but I never thought of courtship as a duty or chore.'

'Then why don't you have yourself a wife and children?'

Mason gave her a serious look. 'Reckon it's because I never met up with a woman like you.'

'Me?' She appeared both flushed and uncertain over his statement.

'I've been a drifter all my life, never willing to put down roots. It's like I was searching for something with no idea of what it was. You know what I mean?'

Lynette appeared to think before answering. When she did, it was a whisper, and there was a distant look in her eyes. 'I believe I do.'

'You're right about my life,' Mason admitted. 'I've

done a lot of fighting and helped folks whenever I could, but I've never belonged to anything or anyone. Since I met you, I've had a yearning deep inside, kind of like there's an empty spot in my heart where there ought to be something more.'

'I think the empty spot is in your head.'

He managed a chuckle at her spunk. 'Reckon you're right.'

For a brief moment, Lynette stared directly into his eyes. The scrutiny was intense and probing. Just as quickly, she averted her gaze and backed up a step.

'I'll fix you something to eat,' she told him abruptly. Then she was gone.

Mason groaned inwardly and reprimanded himself. *Way to go, you slick talkin' devil. Scared her off with one invasive question!*

Dealer and Rutherford were both smouldering with ire. It was Rutherford who spoke first.

'I can't believe you shot him in the back!' He swore vehemently. 'You were supposed to take him on face-to-face.'

Baron Kent lifted his shoulders in a careless shrug. 'Makes no difference if I killed him in a street fight or gunned him down from behind. The man is done and gone. I found the keys at the jail and let everyone out of their cells this morning. Everything's back to normal.'

'Normal?!' Dealer exploded. 'A fair gunfight would have ended it. Shooting the man in the back is going to cause talk and bad blood around town. Not to mention what Lynette will write in the newspaper. What if

73

someone sends for a US Marshal?'

Baron waved a dismissive hand. 'Who has the sand to risk doing something like that?'

'The new mayor for one!'

'Julia ain't the mayor no more. Mike is back in charge, and his two mutts will keep the people in line. If he needs help, I'll lend a hand.'

Rutherford, still fuming, took Dealer's side. 'You told us you could take Mason. The man's hands were probably busted up from his battle with Scraps. He would have been lucky to get his gun free of the holster.'

'The guy wore gloves,' Baron debated. 'As for Scraps, he didn't even hit him. Not once!'

Dealer spat his contempt, the brown liquid from his chaw making a splatter on the floor. It was to make a point, but it prompted a sharp response from Rutherford.

'We got a spittoon in here for a reason. Quit soiling the floor!'

'I'm disgusted, Rudy,' he excused his action. He quickly said: 'I didn't mean to call you by that name, Harve, but I'm fed up with our handling of one lone man. Scraps has bragged endlessly about how he could whup a grizzly with his bare hands. Then he goes out and gets his ears beaten down by a troublesome do-gooder. Next thing, our high-priced top gun sneaks around in the dark like a yellow coyote and back-shoots the man.'

'I never seen anyone hit with the power of that jasper,' Baron remained defensive. 'I mean, you could hear the bones crack when he made contact. Scraps didn't have a prayer against him. The poor devil can't open his mouth more'n a inch or so. Julia said his ribs are cracked and he has a fractured jaw.'

'So that's it!' Dealer taunted the gunman. 'You were afraid Mason was as good with a gun as he was with his fists.'

Baron glared at him. 'I wasn't about to find out. I took the surest route to get the job done!'

'And maybe turned the whole valley against us,' Rutherford growled. 'If you didn't have the guts to face him head-on, you should have hired a couple men to brace him on the street. No one would put up a fuss if the guy died while trying to match guns with two or three men.'

'It's over. Finished!' Baron practically snarled back at them. 'You never questioned how I handled the bank owner!'

'No one knows old man Walters didn't take the buyout offer,' Dealer countered. 'Everyone believed he took the money Harve offered him and left town like a whipped pup. This is different. You killed a man right on the main street of town, a man who was acting sheriff.'

'You two pay me to take care of problems, Dealer. I took care of it!'

Rutherford raised a hand to prevent further arguing. 'We can't undo the damage, but we're going to have to be on alert. Someone might contact the US Marshal's office about the shooting. Plus, we've got a circuit judge headed this way. We have to deal with him too.'

'There's nobody to make any charges against us,' Baron proclaimed smugly. 'With Mason dead, that should be the end of it.'

'Unless your feisty editor decides to testify,'

Rutherford told Dealer pointedly. 'She never believed Walters took the money and left.'

'I'll convince her to keep her mouth shut,' Dealer promised. 'She isn't going to risk having her brother busted up or killed. I'll use him for leverage.'

'We'll leave that to you then,' Rutherford allowed. 'Baron, you stay shed of any trouble. I don't want any more dead bodies to deal with.'

'Yeah, yeah,' he muttered insolently. 'I'll be around when you need me.'

'All right,' Rutherford ended the meeting. 'Don't let on to anyone that you did the shooting.'

Baron snorted: 'You think I'm that stupid?'

'I, for one, never underestimate your God-given talents,' Dealer sallied.

The insult caused Baron to glare at the saloon owner, but he held his tongue and left.

Dealer waited until he was gone to shake his head. 'I always knew that man was more skim milk than cream. This puts us in a hell of a bad light.'

Rutherford shrugged. 'We took over the town without much of a fuss when we first arrived. No one knows we are the Renegades from down Texas way. Besides which, Colorado officials aren't going to care much about warrants from Texas. I had hoped we could take control without any killing, but the banker wouldn't sell.'

'Had better luck with the saloon owner,' Dealer said. 'Baron did scare him off without a fight. He took the money I offered and ran like a scalded cat.'

'We've got a good setup here. Lots of travellers, main stage route, and even the possibility of a railroad spur coming this way. If that happens we'll be rich beyond our dreams.'

His partner grinned. 'I have some pretty fine dreams. Plus, Lafferty and Scraps still work for wages.' Then with a sullen expression: 'And, the day will come when we won't need Baron to stick around.'

'First things first. I know you're hot for the woman editor, but this situation is more important than you making another conquest. We have to make sure there is nothing for the circuit judge to do when he arrives.'

Dealer spat again – hitting the spittoon this time. 'Don't worry, Harve. Everything will be taken care of.'

'There she is!' Wyatt said, pausing at the top of the hill. 'Deliverance.'

'Whoa!' Jared exclaimed, his voice hinged with excitement. 'Looky over there!' He pointed at a ten-foot tall cedar a hundred feet away. 'There's a perfect branch for a hanging. Dad-gum, I've been watching for the last five miles and seen nary a tree that's built for a noose.'

'If I remember right,' Landau quipped dryly, 'you didn't have any trouble hanging those three kidnappers outside of Brimstone.'

Jared grinned. 'I allowed them boys to ask the Lord for forgiveness, but they took to cussing me instead. "Blessed be the Peacemaker",' he quoted from the Bible.

'Peacemaker?' Landau questioned his use of the word. 'You talking about the gun on your hip?'

'No, sir!' Jared cracked. 'I gave each one a chance to make *peace* with the *Maker* before I sent them packin' to Hades.'

'Well, Cousin,' Wyatt said, 'I hate to ruin your day, but that tree limb yonder isn't more than six feet off of the ground. You try stretching someone's neck, he only has to stand on his toes to keep the noose from tightening.'

Jared frowned. 'Well, I reckon we could slip a rope around their ankles and cinch their feet up behind them to their belts.'

'You're one cold fish,' Landau complained. 'It'd be like hanging a man while he was on his knees.'

'If I get holt of the guy who shot Rod in the back, I'll sure 'nuff hang him . . . even if I have to do it from the rafters at the livery stable!'

Wyatt waved a hand to dismiss the subject. 'Let's not gather the eggs before we have any chickens. We have to find out who tried to kill him first.'

'Pretty fair-sized town,' Landau pointed out. 'Take a gander at the two-storey casino – 'pears about as large as the Valeron barn.'

Jared agreed. 'Wide main street for the businesses and houses for two blocks on either side. This town was laid out with a plan for growth.'

'What say, Wyatt?' Landau asked. 'How do we play this?'

The more experienced Valeron gave his head a shake. 'We best take time to figure out what we're up against. We'll slip over to see Mayor Wright, then visit cousin Mason. You keep a low profile; circle around and come in from the other end of town.'

Landau posited, 'I get it. You might need someone to cover your backs, once the people in town know who you are.'

'Yeah. You can pretend to be an out-of-work cowpoke or whatever. Be sure to stay close enough to be around if there's trouble.'

Landau nodded his understanding and turned his horse in the direction of the nearby hills. He began the ride that would allow him to approach Deliverance from the opposite end of town.

Wyatt led the way down to the main street with Jared at his side. Halfway through the busy settlement, they spotted the doctor's shingle and neck-reined their mounts toward his house.

'First time I can recall a town medico being mayor,' Wyatt remarked. 'Most of them don't have time for politics.'

Before they reached the hitch-rail, a ruckus drew their attention a short way down the street. A woman was shouting loudly at a couple of grungy looking fellows. 'Something's happening at the newspaper office,' Jared said. 'Didn't that wire say Mason was helping the town editor?'

'It did. Let's have a look.'

Wyatt and Jared headed their horses that direction and quickly rode over to see what was going on. As they stopped at the front of the building, one of the two men forcibly grabbed a young woman by her arms.

'We're gonna go look-see upstairs and help you pack, Missy!' He snarled the words at her. 'If you want to stay in one piece, you'll not get in our way!'

'You can't storm in here like a couple of vandals!' she cried, struggling against his superior strength. 'Get out!'

The brute wrestled her aside. 'We warned you about

79

interfering before. This time you might end up riding that rail we promised.'

At that moment Wyatt came up behind the two men. He spotted a fancy dressed man sprawled out on the floor, looking dazed, and bleeding from the nose.

'Hold it!' he ordered, drawing his gun. 'What's the trouble here?'

The pair turned on him prepared to fight . . . until they saw the muzzle of his gun pointed in their direction. Choosing not to get holes shot through his favourite body, the one man released his hold on the girl as if he'd taken hold of a hot stove. Both men raised their hands.

The girl didn't tell them what was going on, but hurried to attend to the injured man on the floor.

'Who're you?' one of the pair of ruffians asked. 'And what for are you butting in on something that ain't none of your affair?'

'Name's Valeron,' Wyatt said, 'and we're here to find the man who shot our cousin, Rod Mason.'

'Whoever done the shooting is gonna die!' Jared barked each word sharply, moving up to stand alongside Wyatt. He narrowed his gaze, hand on the butt of his gun, a deadly glow emanating within his eyes. 'Was it one of you? Fess up to it here and now and I promise you a quick death!'

'No! We didn't have nothing to do with it,' squeaked the man who had been grappling with the lady. The colour drained from his face and he took a fearful step back.

'That would be hell no!' said the other, his eyes also wide with fear. 'Me and Connor work for the mayor. We're in charge of keeping law and order around town.'

'Like Sandoval says,' Connor added hastily.

Wyatt harrumphed. 'I suppose your duties include beating up city-slickers and roughing up women?'

'Uh, well, we was ordered to—'

'Shut up, Connor!' Sandoval snapped at him.

'Sorry,' Connor lamented. 'I didn't mean nothing.'

'We was just leaving,' Sandoval, ostensibly the smarter of the two, said carefully. He glanced at the woman. 'Sorry about this misunderstanding, Miss Brooks.'

'You boys lay hands on a lady again,' Wyatt threatened in an ice-cold tone of voice, 'and the next thing either of you see will be the inside lid of the wooden boxes you're being buried in. Savvy?'

'Yes, sir!' Sandoval muttered.

'Like he says,' Connor agreed.

Wyatt stepped aside and allowed the two men to scramble out of the office. They kept up a rapid pace all the way up the street. With the disturbance past, he turned to the woman kneeling on the floor and asked:

'Is the dude you're tending to the newspaper man?'

She raised her eyes intrepidly. 'I am Lynette Brooks, editor and publisher of the *Weekly Herald*,' she informed then firmly. 'This is my brother, Richard. He tried to defend me and ended up on the floor for his trouble.'

'If he needs to see the doctor, we can carry him over there for you.'

'Sandoval only hit him once.' Lynette's tone mellowed. 'Richard is not a fighter.'

Her brother had regained his senses and slowly rose to a sit-up position. 'I should have listened to Mason,' he mumbled through the cloth he was holding to his face.

'But it seemed wholly unmanly to run off and let you face those men alone.'

'Mason!' Jared proclaimed. 'He's the reason why we're here. Is he still alive?'

The girl helped Richard to his feet. As he seemed steady, she paused to take a full measure of the two men who had intervened on her behalf.

'You two are Valeron brothers?'

'Cousins, Miss,' Wyatt replied. 'Most of us Valeron boys share similar features and are on the plain side.'

'You look very . . . comfortable, with a gun in your hand,' she replied carefully, speaking to Wyatt.

'He ought to,' Jared boasted. 'Wyatt is the best man with a handgun in these parts.'

'And you are?'

'Jared Valeron, ma'am.' He grinned. 'Best man at tracking or using a rifle in these parts.'

She could not prevent a simper from surfacing on her lips at his claim. 'As I said, my name is Lynette Brooks, and this is my brother, Richard.' She gestured toward the back of the office. 'Mr Mason is upstairs in my bedroom. We hid the fact that he was alive and hid him until such time as he is able to defend himself.'

'We? Meaning you two and the mayor?'

'The town doctor, actually. The mayor's job reverted back to the crooks running this town the morning after Mason was shot. He was acting sheriff and the short-term mayor was working with him.'

'Sounds a might confusing,' Jared said.

'I'll take you up to see Mason. He can explain the situation to you,' Lynette offered.

'You going to be all right?' Wyatt asked Richard.

'Unless my nose is broken,' he muttered, attempting to stop the irksome trickle of blood. 'That's the first time I've ever been punched in the face. Mason is the only other man who ever hit me . . . and that was to prove a point.'

Wyatt laughed. 'Mason always had a habit of that, even when he was around our side of the family. None of us could ever best him in a fight . . . but it was always in fun.'

'Regrettably, I believe his idea of fun differs dramatically from my own.'

'Follow me,' Lynette said, and led the way up the back stairs.

CHAPTER SIX

Cliff cornered Tish Valeron as she was dispersing the kids for suppertime. She cocked an eyebrow at his approach. He read a warning in her expression. She knew he wanted something . . . and she appeared determined not to give it to him!

Putting forth his best smile, Cliff greeted her warmly. 'You're growing more beautiful every day, Tish. Durned if you don't put the other girls about your age to shame.'

Her answer was succinct. 'The answer is no. N-O. No chance, no way!'

'I haven't asked for anything.'

'You're going to.'

Cliff heaved a worrisome sigh. 'You remember my brother, Rod, don't you?'

The stiff wall of resistance crumbled every so slightly. 'Last time I saw your brother, I had just turned fourteen. He was about the most handsome guy I ever saw.'

'Rodney?' Cliff gasped. 'The guy is tough as horseshoe iron, but handsome?'

'Rugged, manly, virile,' she maintained. 'He reminded me of Brett, or maybe my brother, Troy. They are both pretty big, and they are handsome in their own way.'

'Someone shot Rodney in the back,' Cliff said solemnly, changing tactics. 'Dirty coward didn't dare face him.'

'Yes, I heard about it. Dad said Jared and Wyatt left to help him.'

'It should be me,' he told her tightly. 'I'm his brother . . . and I owe him. I owe him a lot.'

Tish again drew her brows together in suspicion. 'I'm not going to tend Nessy for you.'

'Listen to me, Tish,' Cliff became deadly serious. 'I know most everyone thinks I'm an alley-cat when it comes to chasing girls. I've always been that way. But this has nothing to do with my character; it has to do with a lifelong debt to my brother.'

'What are you talking about?'

'Rodney is the father I didn't have. Our dad was always gone, doing work for the railroad. There were months that went by between visits, due to his job. Rodney took care of both me and Mom. And more than that, he saved my hide from angry suitors, big brothers and even a few fathers. He rescued me from more beatings than I can count.'

'He should have let you take your medicine a few times,' she opined. 'You're like a male hound in season. Every girl on the ranch knows better than to be alone with you.'

'But this is my brother, Tish. If this was Troy or Shane, you'd want to be there for them. Well, this is my chance to give something back for all he has done for me. It's important to me, really important.'

Tish lowered her guard. 'You can't just run off on your own. I've heard that you got lost here on the ranch – more than once! Shane said you don't have any sense of direction.'

'I admit I'm not real good about directions, but Shane is due back at any time. I spoke to your father and he gave the go ahead for me and Shane to ride to Deliverance. But there's a condition.'

'Nessy,' Tish deduced.

'Yes. I can only leave if I can find someone trustworthy to watch Nessy.' The sorrowful look again surfaced. 'I know my adopted daughter likes you. I've seen the two of you together.'

Tish's firm stance wavered. 'She's a little doll, and I admit we get along very well.'

'Then, will you do it?' he pleaded. 'It would only be for a few days, just until we can find out who shot my brother and bring them to justice.'

'That could take weeks, Clifford,' she finally agreed. 'I don't intend to spend my whole summer tending your child.'

'It won't take long,' he promised. 'Wyatt has tamed a town or two, and Jared is the best tracker in the country. Between them, we'll find the person responsible in short order.'

'No more than two weeks,' Tish outlined. 'If the killer is not found in two weeks, you must return home.'

Cliff could not hide his elation. 'I give you my word.'

Tish displayed a sinister simper, dampening his momentary euphoria. 'Oh, it's going to cost you a little more than your word.'

Landau entered the saloon and ordered a beer. Before the bartender could pour him the brew a man sauntered over to the bar next to him. He glanced at the man and recognized him at once.

'Bernie!' he addressed him. 'What're you doing way up here? Thought you never left New Mexico, unless you were on the run.'

Bernie was mediocre looking, dressed in a brown suit that had seen better days, with a fashionable western-style hat tipped back on his head enough to show his thick, wavy, ash-coloured hair. He was an inch or two shorter than Landau, as lean as a fencepost, with a natural grin that won him friends every place he went. His weakness was for cards – he cheated a lot – and often left town one step ahead of a host of angry losers.

'I came to Colorado to change my luck and my occupation,' Bernie said. 'I heard you pulled out of Brimstone to follow a skirt and work on a ranch or something. Did the gal ditch you for something better?'

'Don't think I'm cut out to be tied down to one woman or play nursemaid to a bunch of beef critters. What about you? Any luck with a new career?'

'I landed a good job here at the saloon, in charge of the gambling tables.' He laughed. 'I told the new boss I could spot a cheat a mile off – 'cause I've tried about every underhanded trick there is. He hired me so's I could spot any of our own people – those who gave away they were cheating – along with tin-horn gamblers and card sharps who come through. It keeps me busy enough that I don't have time to gamble on my own.'

'You give up playing cards and it will likely add twenty years to your life.'

He laughed again. 'Yeah, Landau, that's the certain truth.'

Landau got his beer and joined Bernie at his table. They passed the time talking about their days when they were both in the outlaw town of Brimstone. After catching up, Landau questioned him about the saloon owner and the banker. He learned a lot in the next hour and was eager to pass along the information to the Valeron boys. However, he also had to maintain his cover as an out-of-work loner and see what else he could learn.

'Think I might get a job hereabouts?' he queried, when the conversation lagged.

'Dealer Gilmore already has a real hard-case on his payroll. You looking to sell your gun, or are you willing to tend bar?'

'I ain't sociable enough to wait on drunks all night.'

'You decide to work here, I'll put in a good word with Dealer. He might need another man. He and Rutherford pretty much run the whole valley, along with Mike Lafferty.'

'You said that five of them arrived together and took over the town?'

'Yep. Dealer bought the saloon, Rutherford took the bank, and Lafferty ended up with the mayor's post. The other two in their group are a blowhard named Baron Kent – he's the hard-case I mentioned – and a big bruiser name Scraps.' He grunted. 'Scraps was supposed to be the toughest guy around, but he got his head handed to him a couple days back.'

'I hear tell there was a shooting too.'

'Curious, that,' he said meaningfully. 'The man who whupped Scraps was shot in the back the same night. Were I still a betting man, I'd guess Dealer and Rutherford know who pulled the trigger.'

'You think they are behind the drygulching?'

'Dunno for sure. Although a guy rode through a while back who knew a little about their past. He told me they left Texas under a cloud.' He snorted. 'A cloud of dust from the law that was hot on their tails. Dealer called the banker "Rudy" the other day and the banker about come unhinged. Funny reaction when you figure Rudy would be a natural nickname for Rutherford. Anyway, he was mad for a couple days afterward.'

'That is strange.'

Bernie changed the subject. 'You got a place to hang your hat?'

'I still have a little money to tide me over. I'll get a room and stick around town for a couple days.' He grunted. 'Just don't expect me to do any gambling here at the casino.'

'Yeah,' Bernie said. 'I remember you never were much for games of chance.'

'Money's too hard to come by to throw it away on dice or cards . . . especially when I nearly always lose.'

'I hear you,' his friend said. 'Let me know if you want me to check about a job for you.'

Landau shook his hand and walked slowly out of the saloon. He had some suspicions and rumours, but nothing to take before a judge. That would take a little more digging. Thinking about the banker who had up and disappeared – 'digging' might be necessary!

'You sure enough kicked over the milk bucket, tackling this town on your own,' Jared ribbed Mason. 'What did you think would happen?'

'I underestimated the competition,' the wounded man replied. 'Soon as I'm able to get around, I intend to put things right.'

'That's why we're here,' Wyatt told him. 'We intend to lend a hand.'

'Didn't expect a bullet between the shoulders . . . a miscalculation on my part.'

'Wyatt and me will soon set things straight for you,' Jared declared. 'By the time you're on your feet, this will be a town full of pussycats.'

'You ain't changed a bit, Cousin,' Mason spoke to Jared. 'Worst man I ever seen for simply wading into a war with a gun in both fists.'

'Next to you maybe,' Jared joked back.

'He favours a noose nowadays,' Wyatt tossed in his own crack. 'His new motto is "hang 'em all, and let God sort out the guilty".'

'I told Mason about the banker,' Lynette interjected, preventing more playful banter. As she had Wyatt and Jared's attention, she continued. 'I talked to the bank teller and he confirmed my own suspicions. Mort Walters wouldn't have sold out. He loved having his own bank.'

'Any way to check on his background?'

'He once mentioned he had no relatives. Everyone in his family died in an Indian raid. He was attending college at the time. He never married, so there was no one to contact when he went missing.'

'And he hasn't been seen since this gang showed up,' Mason contributed. 'I didn't get a chance to do much investigating, but I'd wager Lafferty knows what happened to the man.'

Lynette continued with what she had learned. 'The teller told me that Connor and Sandoval – the two brutes you met downstairs – cleared Mr Walters' personal belongings from his house. It happens to be the very house where Dealer Gilmore and Rutherford are living now. They added a porch and ice house and have hired an elderly widow to be their cook and housekeeper. The two of them pretty much live like kings.'

'Connor and Sandoval were downstairs?' Mason inquired, immediately concerned. 'You have more trouble with those two grunts downstairs?'

'Richard had them in hand when we arrived,' Wyatt exaggerated. 'We had a few words with them and they left without any trouble.'

'Didn't seem to be the brightest of lamps,' Jared remarked.

'They are objects of brute force,' Lynette confirmed. 'Sandoval is a little smarter than most daisies, while Connor is more on an even keel with a fencepost.'

'We can work with that,' Jared surmised, looking at Wyatt. 'Remember those three coyotes, the ones who stole fifty head of our cattle a year or so back, but we didn't have any proof?'

Wyatt grinned. 'I remember your brother, Reese, telling me about it. You and Shane finagled the rustlers into making confessions.'

'Those skunks couldn't wait for Brett to show up and arrest them,' Jared confirmed. 'They were practically begging him to take them to prison.'

Mason grunted. 'Every time I talk to one of you Valerons, I'm reminded of why I'm glad we're related and not enemies.'

'You concentrate on getting better,' Wyatt said. 'Jared and I will pick up where you left off . . . other than for getting shot in the back.' He laughed. 'We'll try not to repeat that part of your plan.'

As the two Valerons left the room, Lynette gave Mason a worried look. 'Will they be all right? I mean, there were five men who took over this town, and they've added a couple more to their number. I don't see how two men can have much more success than you did alone.'

Mason smiled. 'Miss Brooks, had the Valerons been inclined to join the South during the war, we would likely be living in the Confederate States of America.'

Before the sun set, Mike Lafferty and his two henchmen were back behind bars. Scraps was too stove-up to make a nuisance of himself again, so they let him remain free. Julia assumed the position of interim mayor once more. This time, Lynette printed up a proclamation and posted it on several buildings around town. It stated there would be an investigation concerning the new taxes, the foreclosures of local properties and the disappearance of the banker, Mort Walters. It also announced there would be an election for both mayor and sheriff within a few weeks.

Deciding to conceal the fact Mason had survived the ambush, Wyatt pinned on the sheriff's badge. Jared acted as his deputy and talked to the local businessmen, along with some of the farmers and ranchers. Landau was waiting for Jared when he arrived at the livery, shortly after dark.

'Figured you would show up in time to check on the horses for the night,' Landau greeted him, holding a lamp while he unsaddled his horse.

'Shane would cuss me until crows couldn't fly if I didn't,' Jared replied, putting his horse in the corral. 'He's going to be unhappy when he finds out me and Wyatt left before he got back from the horse sale in Cheyenne.'

As they checked their animals, Landau filled him in about what he had learned and Jared returned the favour. Once they had covered the news, Landau asked: 'Do you and Wyatt want me to actually take a job and work from the inside? Bernie can likely get me hired over at the saloon.'

'We might need you for another chore or two,' Jared answered. 'Best keep your distance until we learn what we're up against. You said the banker got real testy when Gilmore called him Rudy?'

Landau nodded. 'I have a notion about that. It's a story I heard when I was living in Brimstone.' Jared cocked an eyebrow and waited, so he related the details. 'It came from a petty thief who was passing through. He had been down Texas way and said the state's reconstruction was finally taking hold. The new batch of elected officials were reclaiming the towns and cities.

They eliminated the hold-over Yanks and disbanded the black police force, who had been in charge of law and order. Then they commenced to clamp down on corruption and crooks who had taken control of many of their towns. One group to be run out of the country was a bunch called Rudy's Renegades. They went from one place to another, taking over a small town or settlement, and fleecing the people of everything of value, before moving on.'

Jared snorted his understanding and contempt. 'Rudy is Rutherford and the others are his renegades.'

'My conclusion as well,' Landau concurred.

'I'll have Wyatt send a wire or two and see if there are outstanding warrants for these gutter rats.'

'Took care of it already,' Landau said. 'The man running the mail and telegraph office is not a fan of the new tyrants. He cooperates with them, but the new taxes are about to break him. He promised to keep any replies confidential.'

'Glad you decided to tag along,' Jared said. 'Keep snooping, but be careful. These guys have shown their true colours – and it's yellow, down to the bone! Wouldn't want you getting a bullet in the back too.'

'You and Wyatt are the ones taking the biggest chances.'

'Yeah, but we're protected. You're not.'

'Protected?'

Jared laughed. 'Sure, we're Valerons. Who would be dumb enough to kill one of us?'

Landau gave a shake of his head. 'Contrary to your own opinion, everyone might not have heard of the high and mighty Valeron family. Be a shame if you were killed by some ignorant clod who didn't know how important you are.'

'You got a room and money enough for eats?' Jared turned back to their situation.

He gave a tip of his head. 'I'm at the hotel . . . room seven, upstairs.'

'Right. Me and Wyatt are at the jail. Only one cot, but we will sleep in shifts so long as we have prisoners.'

'OK,' Landau said, putting out the lamp. 'I'll be around when you need me.'

Harvey Rutherford was seated behind his desk. An expensive cigar stuck out of the corner of his mouth, resembling a bulldog having fetched a short stick. He didn't fit the executive type, sporting a fair amount of flab, and there was a rusty hue to his nose and cheeks from too much booze. His suit hung on him like a blanket wrapped about a flour barrel, but his shirt had been freshly laundered. As for his hatless head, it revealed a large bald spot at the crown while what hair he had was too long, actually touching his shoulders. He glowered at Wyatt and Jared with insolent agate eyes, furious at their impertinence.

'I understand you have taken three of our townspeople prisoner,' he stated piously. 'On whose authority are you locking up innocent citizens?'

'They're only innocent until proven guilty,' Wyatt countered. 'And there is little chance they will be turned loose.' He narrowed his gaze at the pompous banker. 'You might want to give that some thought.'

'Are you threatening me?'

'Just stating facts. Once those fellows know they are headed for Canyon City, they are liable to start talking.'

Rutherford frowned. 'Canyon City?'

Jared nudged Wyatt's ribs with his elbow. 'Don't you remember, Cuz? This guy hails from Texas. He don't know where the Colorado State prison is located.'

The man's look of displeasure increased. 'Who told you I was from Texas?'

Jared shrugged. 'Word gets around real quick – happens when a bunch of buzzards show up to take over a town. We know you and your fellow gang members hail from down that-away.'

'Yes, well, Texas was getting too crowded,' the banker explained. 'And there's no law against me and a couple of my friends coming to Colorado to start our own business ventures.'

'You picked a place with no lawman.'

'Few towns in this part of the country have a marshal or sheriff. That's why the mayor put a couple of local men in charge of keeping the peace.'

'I've talked to them,' Wyatt said. 'Real top-notch fellows – dull enough of wit to follow about any given order.'

Rutherford snorted. 'What do you want from me?'

'We stopped by to inform you that the law is here to stay, and whoever ordered our cousin to be shot in the back will be forever sorry.'

'*Sorry!*' Jared repeated the word, hedging it in ice. 'Meaning they are going to dangle from a rope, kicking at the wind.'

Rutherford masked total innocence. 'Why tell me?'

'Courtesy,' Wyatt answered. 'We intend to extend the same courtesy to everyone in town. Might even coax one or two of them to start talking.'

'Everything we've done is legal.'

'Assessing a fifteen per cent tax on every business in town, taking over loans that were granted at ten per cent and tripling the interest rate?' Wyatt bore into the man with an accusatory gaze. 'I know a little about the law regarding mortgages. You can't raise a previously agreed-upon interest rate after a loan has been signed. And, as it happens, we have the vice president of a major bank in town; he's offered to audit your records.'

The crook sniffed importantly. 'You can't collect or look at my bank records without a special court order!'

'Mr Colt says different!' Jared spoke up, patting the butt of his gun. 'We are going to place your records in a safe place until the judge arrives. That way, you won't be able to doctor any of the figures.'

'Now see here. . .' he began testily.

Wyatt took a step forward. 'You can hand them over voluntarily, Rudy . . . or we can take them after my cousin leaves you lying face-down and unconscious on the floor!'

Jared smirked. 'Be downright fitting if we treated you the same as your thugs have been treating the local businesses and citizens.'

Rather than get up from his desk, Rutherford made a loathing gesture toward a liquor cabinet. A row of journals were held in place by a couple bookends atop the cabinet. Wyatt picked through them and found the ones he wanted.

'Rest assured, Mr Rutherford,' he told the man. 'We will keep your ledgers safe until the judge and bank auditor finish with them.'

Rutherford gnashed his teeth, red-faced, with veins about to explode from his forehead, but wisely held his silence. He was used to intimidation, but from the other side of the fence. However, he knew better than to resist, restraining himself to simply glowering at the pair with a deadly-hot, molten stare.

As they left the bank, both Jared and Wyatt knew there would be repercussions from their actions. The gauntlet had been dropped and Rutherford was not the sort of man to ignore a challenge.

Julia carefully changed Mason's bandage and asked about his discomfort.

'I reckon I ought to be moving to another room,' he replied. 'You did a good job. There isn't much pain except when I take a deep breath or flex my shoulders.'

'You've got the most muscular back and shoulders of any man I ever treated.'

He grinned at her. 'Comes from beatin' the stuffing out of punching bags ... or rowdies who like to push people around. Never did have the good sense to walk away from a fight.'

'At least you are no longer in this fight alone. I expected someone might come to watch over you, but those two Valeron boys put Lafferty and his two men in jail and reinstated me as mayor ... all within a few hours.'

'Wyatt has tamed a town or two before,' Mason

advised her. 'He knows the steps to take and won't be as careless as I was.'

'Plus, he has a brother to back him up.'

'Jared is his cousin,' he corrected her. 'Tell you true, you could line up the nine Valeron boys and it would be tough to tell which belonged to which of the three families. All of the Valeron fathers carry the same physical traits – passed on down to the boys and even one or two of the girls.'

'Sizable family,' she said, allowing him to button up his shirt.

'You giving me the OK to move to a hotel?'

'You're supposed to be dead. Where can you go that no one will see you?'

'I haven't given it much thought, but I sure do hate putting Miss Brooks out ... 'specially with her brother being in town. Looking after me is taking up too much of her time.'

Julia gave him an odd look, not unlike his mother, when she was worried about him. 'The young lady has a past,' she said softly. 'She confided in me once how a man had done her dirt and left her in disgrace. I don't believe she has gotten over it.'

Mason was surprised she would impart something so private to him. 'She mentioned a little about it to me,' he related. 'And I've noticed she keeps a tight rein on her feelings.'

'That said, I believe she is sweet on you,' the woman told him gently. 'I wouldn't want to see her hurt again.'

He blinked in shock, wondering how he could ever be responsible for bringing pain to someone as precious and special as Miss Brooks. Before he could get his brain working, Julia lightly patted his arm.

'I know you have a good heart, Mason. I'm only suggesting you try and be . . . gentle and understanding. Don't try and move too quickly.'

'Like I said, the injury don't hardly bother me.'

She made a face. 'Not the wound, silly – I'm talking about Lynette.'

He leaned back in momentary confusion. 'Well, yeah,' he muttered inanely. 'That much is clear to me. I've never been ungentle or said a rough word around a lady. As for understanding one, however, I don't have a clue what makes you females tick.'

Julia smiled. 'See? You do understand us.'

Mason remained sitting on the bed as the doctor rotated about and left the room. He paused to scratch his head. *Be gentle and understanding she says . . . 'cept there's no understanding females! Durned if I'm not more perplexed than before her advice!*

CHAPTER SEVEN

Dealer and Baron remained silent while Rutherford stormed about the room, ranting and wildly throwing his arms in the air. 'Me!' he roared between vile cuss words. 'Those two mouthy, cock-a-hoop jokers – talking sass to me!'

'You say they took your record books?' Dealer finally shattered his lengthy tirade.

Rutherford quelled his ire long enough to heave a sigh. 'It shows where I went through and changed all of the interest rates. A judge will see it plain as day. We have to get those journals back.'

'What's the big deal about changing the rates?' Baron wanted to know. 'I mean, most bankers charge whatever rate of interest they want.'

'Yes, but it's against the law to alter a binding contract without the lender agreeing to it,' Rutherford explained patiently. 'It's a form of fraud, and I could end up going to prison.'

'So we take back the books,' Baron suggested. 'There's only two of them.'

'I doubt you'll be able to shoot both of them in the back at the same time,' Dealer jeered. 'And let's not forget, these two are Valerons.'

'So what?'

'I asked around, after they arrested Mike and his boys. Bernie knew a little about them.' The two waited for him to continue, so he clarified what he'd learned.

Baron was stunned. 'You telling us that several Valerons took on the whole murderous stronghold of Brimstone, while there were over a hundred outlaws and gunmen in town?'

'That's what Bernie said. The Valerons ended up killing a couple men, arresting a couple, and hanging three more. One of the Valeron boys is a US Marshal, and Wyatt – the one who is now wearing our sheriff's badge – he killed the Waco Kid in a straight-up shootout.'

Rutherford grunted his admiration. 'I once seen the Waco Kid in action. He was about as quick as any man alive.'

'Well, Wyatt Valeron was quicker.'

'Any idea when the judge is due here?' Rutherford asked Dealer.

'The Brooks gal didn't post a time frame in her latest newsletter, so I'd guess we have a few days yet.'

'What about it, Baron? Got any ideas?' Rutherford wanted to know.

The gunman thought for a moment. 'They likely have the books at the jail, and there is always one of them on guard. It could take a lot of firepower to do this by force.' Even as the words were out of his mouth, he had an idea. 'Of course, there might be another way.'

'I don't relish taking on those Valeron fellows in a head-on gunfight,' Dealer said. 'What have you got in mind?'

Mason was attempting to put on one of his boots when Lynette entered the room. She had a tray with a plate of food and a cup of coffee in her hands.

'What do you think you're doing!' It was a demand not a question.

'I've been a burden to you long enough,' he replied. 'I can serve a purpose by keeping watch over the prisoners, if I move to the jail.'

She set the food and cup down on the nearby dresser and scowled at him. 'You aren't up to standing guard just yet. Look at you – can't even reach down to put your boots on!'

'Miss Brooks, I am sure beholden to you for the care and kindness you've shown, but it isn't right, my being in your room and having you wait on me like a servant.'

'You were shot because you came here to help me. That makes you my responsibility.'

Mason gave her a frank look. 'It's the man who is supposed to be responsible for the woman, not the other way around.'

'That might be true in most instances, but not in this situation.'

'I know you don't trust us men, and there are a good many no woman should ever trust. I speak from experience, because my younger brother is a carousing, no-good skirt chaser. I can't tell you the number of times

I've had to save him from a beating. Truth is, he deserved a good tanning a number of times. He sees women as a conquest, and he's never been true to a single one.'

'But you're different,' she said critically. 'Is that what you're saying?'

Mason didn't reply right away. Instead, he let go of the boot and gingerly reclined back on the bed, not laying down, but relaxed against the propped-up pillow and headboard. Instead of answering her question, he gazed off in remembrance.

'When I was a little boy, my pa brought home a pup. It was about the homeliest mutt you ever saw, but he was my dog. I loved him and he loved me. We were inseparable for better'n ten years. When he died, I cried like a baby.' He paused, somewhat choked up at the memory. 'One summer, when I was fourteen, I worked for a half-breed who rounded up wild horses and broke them to ride. He paid me by allowing I could have my pick of all of the horses we tamed. I chose a little sorrel mare, and she was the best horse a man could want. She come down sick a year or so back and died. I'm not too proud to tell you, full-grown man that I am, I cried over the loss.'

Lynette's expression displayed compassion as she murmured: 'Why are you telling me this?'

'To make a point, Miss Brooks. I'll never have another dog like my childhood friend, and I'll never love another horse as I did that little mare. I reckon I'm a man who invests my feelings wholly and completely when I commit to something. I figure the woman I love will be the same. One dog, one horse, one woman – it's the way I am.'

A curious softness infused Lynette's aspect. She hid the momentary weakness beneath munificent dark lashes and her voice was a mere whisper. 'I . . . I believe you mean that.'

Taking a deep breath, Mason took the next step. 'I'd be right proud to court you proper, Miss Brooks, though I wouldn't want you doing so out of obligation.'

'Mr Mason, I—'

'I swear to you,' he continued, 'that I have a great respect for you, and I'm a man of honour.'

She turned her head slowly from side to side. 'You don't—'

'I further swear that I would never raise a hand to you.'

'Mr Mason,' Lynette spoke more firmly. 'I'm trying to tell you, you deserve someone more worthy than I.'

'Worthy?' He would have laughed at the absurdity, but she had said it in all seriousness. 'I'm a man with a reckless past. I've killed a couple other men, along with a few Indians. And there's been times when I've given a man a beating instead of a warning; I've whupped the fellows who came looking for my brother, Cliff . . . knowing full well that he deserved the punishment. If one of us is not worthy, it's me.'

Her lips pressed together stubbornly. 'But you merit someone innocent, without a sordid past. A girl can only surrender her virtue once, and that should be to the man she is going to marry.'

'If people didn't make poor choices or mistakes, we

wouldn't be human,' he countered. 'I've got my share of blame and guilt to bear. Anyone who has reached our ages is bound to have a few regrets. What I see, when I look at you, is a gal who is as pure as the first glimmer of sunshine on a spring morning, and I'm asking for the chance to court you proper.'

Lynette flicked a quick look at him, meeting his eyes for a brief second. 'Eat your meal and stay in bed,' she said stiffly. 'We can discuss this at another time.'

Mason didn't have a chance to argue that this was a good time. The young lady not only left the room, she closed the door behind her.

'Well, Mason,' he muttered aloud, 'you tossed your hat into the ring . . . and she stomped it flat as a flapjack!'

Dealer called Bernie over to a table in the corner of the saloon. He had a bottle with two glasses on the table, promptly pouring drinks before he began the conversation.

'How is it going?' he asked. 'Any problems I should be aware of?'

'Things are running pretty smooth,' Bernie replied. 'I had to run off a couple gamblers last night – caught them cheating.'

'You're good at your job, Bernie. I appreciate having you work for me.'

'Thanks, boss.'

Dealer got down to the real reason the two of them were at the table. 'I was thinking of the story you told me about the Valerons.'

'Never saw one of them close up before, not until that deputy or whatever he is came in for a beer yesterday,' Bernie replied. He paused to take a sip of the whiskey and noticed it was a much better grade than he was usually served. 'But, yeah, I do know a little *about* them.'

'You said they took on the whole town of Brimstone?'

Bernie had previously relayed the story of how a handful of Valerons and a couple of their hired hands had managed to subdue an entire town. Uncertain what Dealer wanted, he said: 'Yep, they are a family to be wary of. Fact is, I hear the town of Brimstone is downright peaceful and respectable these days.'

'You didn't say why they came after those men. What caused all the trouble?'

'The head honcho over all of Brimstone had a brother who was about as smart as your average June bug. He kidnapped one of the Valeron girls and killed her husband-to-be in the process. He and every man-jack involved was either hanged or shot, including the Waco Kid.'

'*Kidnapped?*' Dealer's voice cracked like a teenager on the verge of puberty. 'You said kidnapped?'

'Yeah,' Bernie chuckled at the notion. 'Like I said, that idiot brother didn't have a brain in his head. No one but a complete moron would grab a Valeron. Their family has a US Marshal and a dozen fighting men in their number. If the devil himself ever crossed one of them, I wager he'd skedaddle back to hell in one big hurry.'

Dealer didn't say a word, but rose from the table so quickly he knocked over his chair. A wild look was on his face as he rushed out of the room.

'What the deuce did I say?' Bernie asked aloud, staring after him in wonder.

Jared had an idea for finding out the assumed-dead-banker's location and was searching for a quiet spot a short way from town. He happened to be in a cove, surrounded by enough chaparral that he and his horse were hidden. That is when he spotted the two riders. A couple of drifters would not have drawn his attention, but this pair was leading a third saddled horse. The horsemen were dirty, unshaven, with nearly shapeless hats from the elements, packing pistols and full ammunition belts around their waists and rifles in scabbards. They moved warily, looking this way and that, plus continually watching their back trail. Approaching town from the hilly side, with no main trail to follow, they were apparently sneaking into town from the least visible angle.

His first inclination was they might be going to try and break someone out of jail, but why only one extra horse? There were three inmates behind bars. He decided to keep an eye on them and remained hidden by the brush until they had gone well past his position. Then he mounted up and began to follow along.

His hunch paid dividends. The two men went through an alleyway and tied off their horses behind the newspaper office. They tried the rear door but it was bolted from the inside. Jared waited as the pair slipped around the building to the front, before he dismounted his horse. With gun in hand, he moved quickly through the passage to come in behind the two men. An extra horse meant they intended to take someone with them. As only the doctor and the Brooks knew Mason was alive, it stood to reason the target was either the woman or her brother. Likely, the duo either planned to use one of them as a hostage to trade for the three prisoners or in exchange for ransom.

Even as Jared reached the main street another man appeared. He had a gun out and was rushing toward his position. He waved at Jared and pointed towards the editor's office.

'It's kidnappers!' he called just loud enough for Jared to hear him. 'They're after Richard Brooks!'

Jared didn't recognize this guy, but he nodded his understanding of the situation. The two of them arrived at the doorway in time to see the pair of gunmen inside. One had Richard by the arm and the other had his gun pointed at Lynette.

'Hold it!' Jared shouted.

But the man at his side opened fire, putting two bullets in the man holding Richard. The second outlaw swung around to shoot back, but Jared was quicker, putting a slug through his heart before he could get off a round. In the blink of an eye, two men lay dead on the floor.

Jared moved promptly forward and checked for signs of life. They would learn nothing from either outlaw. He holstered his gun and scrutinized the man who had fired first.

'We might have taken them alive,' he said.

'It's the Barkley boys,' the trigger-happy gent answered back, also putting away his gun. 'One of the men at the saloon overheard them talking. He said they were going to grab Lynn's brother and trade him for Mike Lafferty and his boys. I imagine Lafferty would have paid handsomely for their freedom.'

'And who might you be?'

'Dealer Gilmore,' he replied. 'I own the saloon and have a vested interest in Lynn's welfare.'

'It is a one-sided interest,' she clarified, remarkably composed after such a traumatic experience. 'I thank you for your help, Mr Gilmore, but I'm certain Mr Valeron could have handled this by himself.'

'How did you happen to show up at the right time?' Dealer asked Jared. 'I only just learned about their plan.'

'I seen the pair heading for town with an extra horse in tow. Looked like troublemakers to me so I followed them.'

'Very astute of you,' Dealer commented. 'I hadn't heard of your family, but my floor manager knew something about you. It would seem the Valeron reputation for law and order is warranted.'

'W-what about these two dead men?' Richard, still trembling from the attack, spoke for the first time. 'They are . . . cluttering up my sister's workplace.'

A number of people had gathered on the street, having been drawn to the shooting. Jared motioned to the crowd.

'Would some of you fellows lend us a hand with these two?' he asked no one in particular.

Several men filed inside the room and they carted the bodies off to the coffin maker. Then Jared shooed the rest away, assuring the spectators that the newspaper would put out the story in detail.

Dealer was standing next to Lynette when Jared turned his attention back to her. Richard had recovered his wits, quickly becoming more accustomed to violence. He forced a smile at Jared.

'I must admit, I've been involved in more fights since I arrived in Deliverance than I've encountered in my entire life.'

'There's usually sparks flying when the law comes to a wide open town,' Jared informed him. 'Wyatt has tamed more than one place like this, and it always took his guns and fists to get the job done. Can't have steak without someone butchering the beef.'

'Lynn, are you sure you're all right?' Dealer asked the lady.

'We're unharmed, Mr Gilmore. Thank you again for joining in to stop Richard's abduction.'

'I'm always available should you need me,' he replied deliberately, eying her like a love-starved puppy. 'You know you only have to give a holler, should you need anything at all.'

'I'm sure we'll be fine,' she said more forcefully. 'Excuse me now, I must clean up the blood and write this story for tomorrow's edition.'

He displayed a warm smile. 'Certainly, Lynn.' Then he averted his eyes to Jared. 'Nice to meet you, Mr Valeron. With that second man standing so close to the lady, I'm glad you're a good shot.'

'Appreciate your help,' Jared said in return.

As soon as he left, Richard closed the door. Lynette picked up a rag, ready to clean up the blood on the floor, when she stopped and gaped at the stairway.

'Mason!'

He was standing there, wearing only his pants, with a bandage wrapped about his chest and a gun in his hand. He was ashen from the physical exertion, but had managed to make his way to the landing.

'I . . . I heard shooting.'

'Some hero you are,' Jared snickered. 'You're about five minutes late, if you were intending a rescue.' His voice might have been teasing, but he hurried up the stairs and slipped a supportive arm around his cousin. 'Best get back to bed,' he directed seriously. 'You're stove-up enough that I reckon I could take you in a fight. Just kick back and relax. Me and Wyatt have got a handle on things.'

'Sounds good.' Mason sighed. 'I feel about as weak as a newborn lamb.'

Jared laughed heartily. 'Never figured to hear those words come from your lips, Cuz . . . and that's the truth.'

Rutherford and Baron were both aghast, hearing what had happened.

'You killed the Barkleys?' Baron sounded off in disbelief. 'But . . . damn! You had me hire them to do the job!'

Dealer glared at him and snapped: 'You got sand for brains, Baron!'

'Now hold on!' He was instantly miffed. 'You thought this was a good idea when I come up with it. You agreed to the plan!'

'That was before I talked to Bernie at the saloon. You remember his story about the Valerons making a name for themselves by taking on the town of Brimstone?' At Baron's nod, he went on: 'Well, the reason they went to that bandit stronghold was because several of those bandits stole a girl on her wedding day – a Valeron bride-to-be!' He let the words sink in. 'Men from that family took on a hundred gunmen to get their kin back, all because she was kid-napped by some dolt who probably didn't know who she was. If we had taken Brooks, the Valerons might have called in their brothers and cousins to wipe us out. Think about that!'

Rutherford grunted his agreement with Dealer. 'The dozen or so men we could gather for a fight would have little chance against the men who brought down an outlaw stronghold.'

Dealer exhaled slowly to calm his ire. 'I tried to get there in time to stop it, maybe warn off the Barkley boys without a fight. But Jared Valeron got there at the same time. I had to silence them both before they could point a finger at us.'

'You did what you had to do,' Rutherford praised his deed. 'Good thing you found out in time.'

'Maybe so,' Baron opined. 'But this ain't sounding so good. How are we going to deal with these guys if they have a dozen vindictive relatives ready to come after us?'

'It has to look like a fair fight,' Dealer said. 'Get them to commit to a gun battle with several men, so we are not involved.'

'Coulda' hired the Barkley brothers, if they weren't being fitted for wooden boxes about now,' Baron remarked sourly. 'According to the barkeep, they were here to meet up with a few friends.'

'This could still work,' Rutherford said, thinking fast. 'We don't have to tell their pals that Dealer took a hand in their demise. Far as anyone knows, Valeron killed the two brothers in cold blood.'

'I like it!' Dealer was enthusiastic. He looked at Baron: 'Who were they supposed to meet?'

'The Barkleys were part of Three-finger Markum's gang,' Baron said. 'The bartender said they often come here between jobs to relax – never any lawmen around this part of the country. It's how I knew they would agree to do the kidnapping.'

'Three-finger Markum,' Dealer repeated the name. 'How many men does he have?'

'Sounded like a half-dozen or more, meaning four or five in the bunch with Markum. That ought to be enough to handle two gunmen.'

Rutherford rubbed his hands together with anticipation. 'Yes, yes, and they will want revenge on the man who killed the Barkley boys. We only have to make sure your name doesn't come up.'

Dealer gave his endorsement to the idea. 'I'll have Bernie keep an eye out for them. When they show up, Baron can sic them on the Valerons.'

'Make certain they know what they're up against,' Rutherford told Baron. 'Those two Valerons won't be easy to beat.'

Baron agreed. 'I'll tell Markum to set up an ambush. With the right planning, both Valerons will be dead before they have a chance to draw.'

'They can do it any way they want,' Dealer said. 'But

warn them to make it look like a square shoot. We don't want any more trouble over the killing of Rod Mason. This needs to end.'

CHAPTER EIGHT

Julia frowned at Mason as Lynette looked on. 'Started the bleeding again with your valiant act of trying to stop the kidnapping,' the doctor criticized his actions.

'Couldn't even make it all the way down the stairs,' Mason confessed.

Lynette injected: 'He would have been killed, had he burst in on those two gunmen. It was a foolish thing to do.'

'Take my word for it,' Mason avowed, 'had I gotten there in time, I would have stopped them. They might have finished me off, but I'd have taken them with me.'

'Save me from heroes,' Julia retorted dryly. 'I'm sure you would have prevented the kidnapping, but you would have ruined my considerable effort to save your life. What kind of gratitude is that?'

Mason grinned. 'I'll thank you now, in case the same type of situation comes up again.'

'Men!' Lynette declared, allowing the exasperation to enter her tone.

'How can you risk throwing away your life in such cavalier fashion?'

116

'There are things in this here world worth dying for, Miss Brooks,' he retorted. 'You being at the top of my list.'

'Done,' Julia said, before any further conversation could continue. She stepped back from having finished with the new bandage. 'You need at least three more days in bed, before you go out to save the world. Is that understood?'

'Yes, ma'am,' Mason replied. 'I'm beholden to you.'

'Talk me into becoming mayor and then you go and get yourself shot,' she reminded him. 'I don't intend to clean up the mess you started alone.'

'No, ma'am,' Mason replied.

'So do as I say,' she finished. Then regarding Lynette with a critical stare, 'I'm holding you responsible. You keep that man in bed until he can walk under his own power . . . without tearing open the wound in his back!'

Soon as Julia left the room, Lynette fixed Mason with a hard countenance. 'See what you did? You got both of us in hot water.'

'I heard the commotion downstairs,' Mason excused his actions. 'I couldn't lie here and do nothing.'

She relaxed her staunch posture and sighed. 'I understand. It was a foolhardy thing to do, but you couldn't help yourself.'

'It's bad enough to be occupying your bed,' Mason said. 'But having you waiting on me day and night?' He shook his head. 'I've never been in debt to a woman – unless you count my mother for bringing me into this world. It's hard for me to deal with.'

'I suppose it would be different if you were at Julia's house.'

'No, it wouldn't,' he contradicted. 'I've never owed a debt I haven't paid. With her, I can fork over a few dollars for her services, being that she's a doctor. There's no way I can repay you.'

Lynette heaved a sigh and sat down on the edge of the bed. She rotated her upper body until she was looking directly at Mason.

'Need I remind you? I'm the reason you were shot.'

'My being too cocksure got me a bullet in the back.'

'Yes, well, Richard brought you here to help me, so I'm still responsible.'

The two sat in silence for a time, each with their own thoughts. Mason was first to break the strain.

'Durned if you aren't the most beautiful woman I've ever been this close to,' he said in a husky voice. 'I'd die a thousand deaths just to hold you in my arms one time.'

His declaration caused Lynette to stiffen her back and suck in her breath. 'Mason!' she gasped.

'I mean it, Miss Brooks. The first time I laid eyes on you, you up and stole my heart. I can't think of anything but you.'

'But . . . Mason,' her voice was soft, yet ambivalent. 'I . . . I'm not. . . .'

She didn't finish, as a gentle hand cupped the back of her neck. Even as she was rotating her head in a negative gesture, she allowed Mason to pull her to him so their lips could meet. Hesitant, uncertain, the contact was nonetheless tender and gratifying for them both.

Cliff rushed out to the barn to meet Shane, reaching his cousin before he had managed to unsaddle his horse.

He told him about his brother being shot and how he wanted to ride for Deliverance. Shane listened intently and was eager to go. His enthusiasm stalled, with a stern expression entering his make-up.

'What about your little girl?' he wanted to know. 'Has Uncle Locke agreed to let us make the trip?'

'I had to talk Tish into watching Nessy, but yeah, he gave the OK.'

Shane narrowed his gaze. 'Tish isn't usually anxious to tend kids. Being the baby of all of us Valerons, she's barely past needing someone to tend her.'

'Your youngest sister is a blackmailing sidewinder!' Cliff clarified. 'But we reached an agreement.'

'Yeah? What kind of agreement?'

'I have to give her half my daily wages for each day we are gone.'

Shane laughed heartily at the news.

'Besides that,' Cliff lamented, 'she demanded ten dollars extra, in advance, so she could take Nessy to town to do some shopping. She thinks I haven't provided enough decent clothes for my little orphan.'

'That's my little sister.' Shane grinned. 'Tish has always been money conscious.'

'I'll be pinching pennies for months,' Cliff admitted. 'Sure wouldn't want to be the guy who takes her for a wife.'

'You could have asked Darcy.' Shane mentioned his other sister, still living at home. 'Unlike Tish, she can be dealt with.'

'She's staying in town for a few weeks, working with Brett and Desiree. They are putting together the necessities for a town charter. Don't know what all she has to do with it, but Darcy has always been good with numbers and writing.'

'She's the smart one in our family,' Shane concurred. Then he asked: 'Any news from Jared or Wyatt so far?'

'Nothing yet, but they've only been gone a coupla days,' Cliff replied. 'What do you say? Are you ready to go with me?'

'Try and stop me!' Shane declared. 'I'll need a few minutes to get something to eat. I had hoped to make it home before breakfast.'

'You eat and I'll get the horses ready to go.'

'Did you already settle up with Tish?'

'Locke is in on the agreement – at your sister's insistence! He'll give her the money and deduct it from my pay.'

Shane grinned. 'Did he rib you about letting Tish get the better of you?'

'Not in so many words, but his eyes were laughing out loud!'

'Cliff,' Shane grinned, 'for a hound who used to woo everything wearing a skirt, you have become a family pet. Nessy runs you ragged, and now Tish has you giving her money and doing her bidding. If you're not careful, you're going to become as housebroke as the family cat.'

'Aw, go stuff some chow in that big mouth of yours!'

Shane continued the mirth. 'Rod would laugh himself sick if he knew about this setup.'

'Hurry up!' Cliff barked the order. 'I've already got supplies packed for the trip.'

'Saddle Domino for me,' Shane instructed. 'He's in the corral back of the barn. Which mount are you taking?'

'Bonnet,' he replied. 'She's got the stamina for a hard ride.'

'Good choice,' Shane approved, starting for the house. He cocked his head and called over his shoulder: 'Meet you out front in fifteen minutes.'

It was early afternoon and the saloon only had a few patrons, mostly town drunks, a lone card player, and a couple men waiting for the stage. Landau's eyes adjusted to the dark interior lighting and he was surprised to see Bernie was the fellow at the table. He wandered over and pulled out a chair.

'Didn't figure you to keep such early hours, being that you are up until closing time every night.'

Bernie's eyes were red from lack of sleep, but he managed a weary smile. 'Special duty today, keeping watch for the boss.'

'He go somewhere?'

'Not that I know of. I'm keeping a lookout for Three-finger Markum and his men.'

'Never heard of him.'

Bernie shrugged. 'He's small-time, most often rustles a few head of cattle or horses.'

'Your boss think he might try and run off a few bottles of red-eye, or swipe a keg of beer?'

That brought a chuckle. 'Actually, he wants his gun hand, Baron Dent, to be the one to tell them about the Barkley brothers. I'd wager that's so he can be sure his own involvement isn't part of the story.'

'I heard about the shooting,' Landau said. 'I can tell you one thing, I sure wouldn't go after anyone the

Valerons are protecting.'

Bernie looked around, making certain no one was within ear-shot. 'If I was a bettin' man – like I used to be – I'd wager my next month's earnings that Dealer intends to sic Markum on the Valerons.'

'Be a quick way for them to join their pals in the bone yard,' Landau said, careful to hide his keen interest.

'I don't like the idea one bit,' Bernie confided. 'Something smells to high heaven about this whole thing. I mean, how did the Barkleys think kidnapping Brooks would get them a pile of money? After all, the guy works at a bank, but that doesn't mean anyone is going to fork over a wad of cash to save his hide. Not to mention, the bank is several hundred miles away. And, if they intended to exchange him for Lafferty, who would pay? Lafferty earns his keep as mayor, but he doesn't have the money of Dealer or Rutherford. Besides, what would keep the ex-mayor from being tossed right back in the hoosegow, if he was traded for Brooks?'

'You're right, Bernie. This deal has the aroma of a hermit's outhouse.'

'Another thing,' the casino manager continued his inquest, 'how did they learn about Brooks himself so quick? Until he showed up, I didn't even know the lady editor had a brother.'

'I happened to arrive just after the shooting,' Landau told Bernie. 'I overheard Jared Valeron say he saw the two Barkleys approaching town from the hills. He was suspicious because they had an extra saddled horse and were sneaking around. How is it that Dealer showed up at the same time?'

'There's another puzzle,' Bernie said. 'Dealer was sitting at my table and we was talking some. Then he suddenly jumps up and runs out of the saloon. A minute later, there are shots from down the street. How the devil did he know what was going on? He was facing me, with his back to the street.'

Landau knew Bernie was basically honest, except when playing cards for money. He decided the man could be useful and was in the perfect position to keep his eyes and ears open.

'Listen to me,' he spoke in a quiet, earnest tone of voice. 'I don't want it known just yet, but I'm a friend of the Valerons.' He watched for a reaction, but Bernie showed only a keen interest.

'We think Dealer and Rutherford killed the banker,' Landau informed him. 'And Mike Lafferty has been exhorting money from the businesses since taking over as mayor. I sent a wire to the law in Texas, and found out there are outstanding warrants for Rutherford and all four of his pals.'

'So what does this have to do with the kidnappers?'

'That much doesn't make sense. If Dealer hired or encouraged them to do the job, why would he show up to kill one of them?'

A light of understanding entered Bernie's eyes. 'Hot-damn!' he said firmly. 'I think I know the answer to that!' And he explained how he had just commented to Dealer about the reason the Valerons took on the town of Brimstone – due to a kidnapping of one of their kin.

'Makes perfect sense,' Landau applauded his logic. 'It all fits, right down to you trying to set up a meeting with

Markum. Dealer wants to avoid any blame for the Barkley brothers' deaths.'

'I reckon we're right on track,' Bernie said. 'This is fixing to be one big mess.'

'Unless you and I intervene.'

Bernie's eyebrows arched with a incisive interest. 'What do you have in mind?'

'You play this hand right,' Landau told his friend, 'and you'll either end up dead or running this place.'

The statement put a frown on his face. 'Don't go shovelling sugar with your proposal. Getting dead don't interest me none. But,' he added quickly, '*running* this saloon definitely has my attention!'

Jared entered the sheriff's office to find Julia and Wyatt standing at the desk, watching Richard go over the bank records. Julia offered a smile in greeting, while Richard continued to study the ledger in front of him.

'Interest fraud will be a snap to prove,' Richard announced. 'Rutherford didn't bother to cover his tactics. He simply incorporated a new interest rate on every loan on the books. The payment remained the same, but hardly anything was deducted from the principal amounts. Anyone who signed a contract or loan agreement with Walters will have a case against him.'

When Richard finished explaining his findings, Wyatt asked Jared: 'What's up?'

'Trouble.'

Wyatt pulled a face. 'Can't you ever bring good news?'

'Landau just told me that Three-finger Markum is in

town, Cuz. He arrived with four men and is going to come gunning for us. Especially me.'

'Five of them, huh?' Wyatt frowned. 'That could pose a problem.'

'Landau thinks they will set up a trap. I told him to stay out of sight and do whatever is necessary to even the odds, if it comes to a fight.'

'What on earth is fair about five against two?' Julia wanted to know.

'Three!' Richard corrected.

Wyatt began to check the loads in his Colt. 'I'm guessing they don't know Dealer was involved with the killing of the Barkleys.'

'Landau said Dealer's gunnie, Baron Kent, is the one who spoke to Markum. You can bet he claimed I did the shooting.'

'They won't take us on while we're in here. I'd guess they will wait until we are outside and vulnerable to attack from a door or window.' Wyatt shrugged. 'From what we know of them, they are rustlers and bandits. I don't expect them to try us head on, not even with five against us two.

'Three!' Richard put in a second time.

'You have to watch the jail,' Wyatt told him. 'Rutherford might try to send someone here to break out his pals, while we are busy dealing with Markum and his men.'

'I can watch the jail,' Julia volunteered.

'We won't risk your life, Mayor. We might need you to patch one of us up.'

'What's the play, Wyatt?' Jared inquired, having also

checked his gun. 'You're the one with experience as a town tamer.'

'If we don't show ourselves, Markum might grab Miss Brooks or even a store owner to force us out into the open.'

'On the other hand, they might simply challenge you on the main street of town,' Julia remarked positively, looking past Jared and out the single front window.

Wyatt took a step around the desk so he could see clearly. 'I hope Landau isn't taking a nap. There's only three of them out there.'

'Makes it look like a fair fight,' Jared observed. 'Fair, that is, if you consider the two of us against three of them.'

'The other two are no doubt lying in wait, probably with rifles.'

Julia said: 'You don't have to step out in the open. Make them come to the front of the building; don't give a sniper a clean shot.'

'We'll wait until they call us out,' Wyatt made the decision. 'That should give Landau a chance to get in a position to help against the two missing assailants.'

Jared bared his teeth, squelching his ire. 'Dirty, lowdown rat-maggots! Five of them against two of us, yet they don't have the guts to take us on without a couple hidden shooters! Any we don't kill outright, I'm gonna hang!'

'You certainly have a hankering to stretch a man's neck,' Wyatt teased. 'I sometimes wonder what Uncle Locke missed in your upbringing.'

'He often read to us from the Good Book,' Jared

quipped back. 'You know the part I remember best – "an eye-for-an-eye".'

'What about turning the other cheek?' Julia queried.

'Mayor,' Jared said dryly, 'I don't think that sentiment was intended for anyone living west of the Missouri river.'

Wyatt grinned, but remained deadly serious, mentally preparing for a life and death encounter. 'Test your holster,' he instructed Jared. 'Make sure your gun comes out easy. If this turns to gunplay, don't hesitate.' Sternly, his voice as cool as a January breeze, 'And don't try anything fancy, like trying to hit your target in the shoulder or gun hand. In a stand-up gunfight, you shoot to kill, and keep shooting until your opponents can't return fire.'

'I'm with you, Cuz,' Jared returned, his aspect a mask of earnest concentration. 'I've never been in a scrap like this before, but you can count on me.'

Lynette looked up from editing an article as Landau rushed through the door. 'We need to get Mason out of bed!' he exclaimed, out of breath.

'Mason? Who are—'

'Lady,' he interrupted hastily, 'I came here with the Valeron boys. There's a gunfight coming and I need Mason's help. I mean like right now!'

'Yes! All right!' she declared emphatically, accepting his word. 'Tell me what you need.'

'There's two shooters setting up to bushwhack Jared and Wyatt. I'll take care of the one on the roof of the mercantile store, but the second one is across the street, in the alleyway between the barber shop and the cafe. Mason has got to get around behind him and stop him from getting off a shot. From atop the building where I'll be, I won't be able to cover both men at the same time.'

'I'll get him there. I promise!'

'Hurry!' was his last word, as he spun about and raced back out the door.

Lynette took the stairs two at a time and burst into the bedroom. Mason had been asleep, but her sudden entrance awakened him.

'What is it?' he asked, making an attempt to sit up. He grit his teeth and strained to rise, using both hands to push himself to a sitting position.

She took one look and knew he would never get dressed, out of bed, down the stairs, and then across the street and around a building or two in time to help the Valerons. She grabbed his gun from its holster, which had been hooked over the bedstead.

'Is this weapon ready to fire?'

Mason stretched out a hand, as if he would try and stop her. 'What's going on?'

'Is it ready to shoot?' she shouted sternly.

'Yeah,' he replied. 'Just cock the hammer back and pull the trigger. It's got six loads ready to fire. But what—'

Without a word of explanation, Lynette swirled about and sped from the room.

CHAPTER NINE

Three men, dressed in cow puncher garb, had their hands on the butts of their guns, primed for a gunfight. As they approached down the centre of the street, the people, sensing what was about to happen, cleared the sidewalks. Spectators took up viewpoints from the shelter of nearby businesses, none of them wanting to get hit by a stray bullet.

'Jared Valeron! I'm Three-finger Markum.' The one in the centre ejected the words like a growling dog. 'Yuh killed two of our friends. Come on out and take yore medicine!'

Wyatt pushed the door open, paused for a moment, then exited the sheriff's office. He took only one step and stopped, regarding the trio of men with a critical eye.

'I'm Sheriff Wyatt Valeron, the law in this here town. You start any trouble, Markum, and I'll toss the lot of you in a cell.'

'Wyatt Valeron.' The man sneered the name. 'Yeah, we done heard of yuh. Big man with a gun is the story.'

'The Barkleys were trying to kidnap one of our citizens,' Wyatt told him. 'If they hadn't been killed in the act, I'd have dragged them before a judge and they would have hanged. That's the law in this country – kidnapping is a hanging offence.'

'Talk don't change nuthen,' Markum drawled. 'Killin' our friends be a dying o'fence.'

Wyatt issued a second warning: 'Up till now, the only wanted poster on your gang is for rustling cattle. If me and Jared step out to meet you, we will have no option but to kill the three of you.'

'Yuh talk real big, law-dog,' Markum scoffed. 'Reckon yuh can tell yore story tuh the devil. We aim tuh put yuh toes-up, with a shovel full o' dirt in yore faces.'

Jared moved out next to Wyatt and spoke under his breath. 'You think Landau has had time to take out the two other shooters?'

'The polite conversation seems to be over,' he answered back. 'Guess we'll soon find out.'

'Landau lets us get killed,' Jared muttered grimly, 'and he'll never win Scarlet's favour. I've always been her favourite brother.'

'Small comfort, if we end up dead.'

'Which one is my meat?'

'I'll take Markum and the one on his right. You take the one on the left and then help out if I need you.'

'Let's get to it, Cuz.'

Wyatt started forward, with Jared in step with him at his side, facing the trio of gunmen. They didn't get too close, stopping sixty feet away – near enough to hit their target, yet far enough to force their opponents to take aim. He and Jared readied themselves, both in a gunman's crouch, hands over their guns, ready to kill or be killed.

'Don't fret the rifleman up here, Sheriff!' Landau's voice sounded off from a short way off. 'He's out of the fight.'

Markum stiffened at the news and cocked his head to glance upward at the mercantile roof. Before he could react to losing one of his ambushers, there came another shout, that of a woman.

'Same over in the alley, Sheriff! I got this one!'

Wyatt grinned his satisfaction. 'All right, Markum. It's almost an even fight. You want to drop your irons, or do we kill the three of you?'

Markum didn't pause to consider options, he cemented his fate – making a desperate grab for his six-shooter!

Jared considered himself a fair hand with a gun, but he barely cleared leather before Wyatt's pistol had fired twice. Fortunately, Jared's antagonist had been caught flatfooted by Markum's sudden reaction, making him a tad slow to react. The result: Jared's first bullet hit him in the chest, followed by a second slug that ripped a path through his heart.

Wyatt had taken Markum with such quickness that the man next to him didn't try to draw. Instead of reaching for his gun, he reached skyward, throwing his hands up in the air. From such a pose, he watched Markum crumble to the ground.

'Don't shoot!' he cried. 'I ain't no gunfighter.'

'Who put you up to killing us?' Wyatt demanded to

know. 'Who hired you?'

The frightened man shook his head. 'We was aiming to get even for the Barkley brothers. A guy told us Jared Valeron done the shooting. Far as I know, weren't no one trying to hire us for anything.'

As Wyatt considered the news, Landau appeared with a man under his gun. From across the street, Lynette herded a second one their direction.

'Jail is getting pretty full,' Jared remarked. 'I think we ought to hang these three.'

'Attempted murder is not usually a hanging offence,' Wyatt replied. 'We'll put Lafferty in with his loser cohorts and let the three of them take turns sleeping on the two cots. Reckon these rustlers can do the same. I'm guessing they will serve some time for cattle theft. Plus, we can add this foiled ambush to their sentencing.'

Jared sighed dejectedly. 'Be a sight easier all around to string 'em up.'

'If ever you get tired of being the hunter for the family, you can sure enough become a professional hangman.'

Landau took over watching Lynette's man and gave her a stern look. 'You were supposed to send . . .' (not wanting to mention his name aloud) 'that friend of yours to take care of this sidewinder.'

'He would have been too late,' she informed him curtly. 'I didn't dare waste time looking around for someone else to help out.'

'We're beholden to you, Miss Brooks,' Wyatt spoke up. 'One or both of us might be dead if you hadn't taken a hand.'

'I'm the one responsible for starting this conflict,' she said. 'Helping you is the least I can do.'

'Better get back to your office,' Jared told her. 'Someone might have overheard the shooting and be worried about you.'

Lynette gave a bob of her head and hurried off in the direction of her newspaper and apartment.

'Looks like your undercover work is out in the open,' Wyatt told Landau. 'Round up a couple townsfolk and get these two bodies off of the street. We'll put these three in a cell and hope the circuit judge arrives before we arrest anyone else.'

Landau accepted the order without question. 'You're the boss, Wyatt. I'll check in with you after we plant these two in the cemetery.'

Lynette arrived to discover Mason fully dressed and sitting on the chair she had been using at his bedside. He was in the process of pulling on his second boot. She glowered at his efforts and gestured with the gun in her hand.

'You get back to bed this instant!'

Mason grimaced at the effort but rose to a standing position. 'Miss Brooks, I'm not going to sit by and let you risk your life in my place. What did you think you were doing, taking my gun and running off that way? What was the shooting I heard?'

She took a moment to replace the pistol in his holster before answering. 'It was nothing. Your cousins needed a little support to deal with the Markum gang. Wyatt and Jared had to kill two of them.'

Mason moved to stand closer, regarding her with a severe stare. 'You might have gotten hurt.'

'Had I not have acted in your place, one or both of your cousins might have been killed.' She was unapologetic. Nevertheless, her expression softened, as she gazed into his eyes. 'I was in no danger.'

'But it's my job, not yours,' Mason maintained, struggling to keep his voice austere. 'It's up to the man to do the fighting, to protect the women and children.'

'I've not had anyone take care of me since I was a child,' she murmured.

'Well, you hadn't met me yet,' he replied awkwardly. 'I'd like the honour of taking care of you. And, in return, you can take care of me too.' Then he frowned. 'But, when it comes to handling a gunman or rowdy – that's my job.'

Rather than argue the point, Lynette rose up on her toes and placed a gentle kiss on his lips. 'I won't do it again. I promise.'

'Miss Brooks . . .' he attempted to speak. 'I have to—'

'Lynette,' she whispered, kissing him a second time. 'Call me Lynette.'

Mason prided himself with being as tough as most any other man, but this girl . . . this delectable, charming, beautiful young woman. . . .

Durned if her kisses aren't sweeter than honeycomb, he thought.

When her arms went around him, he responded in kind and forgot everything but her.

It was a council of war meeting between Rutherford, Dealer and Baron. The mood was not a jovial one.

'Who would of thought the Brooks woman would interfere?' Baron complained. 'And who the hell was that other guy?'

Dealer answered: 'Bernie said the fella was looking for work, but he was in Brimstone when the Valerons cowed the entire town. He must have taken their side in the fight because he knew them.'

'The good news,' Rutherford said, 'is that Markum never mentioned any of us. He and his men were intent on getting even for the death of the Barkley boys. That means we are in the clear on this.'

'Yeah, Rudy,' Dealer said thickly, 'but it don't change anything about you altering the contracts and upping the interest rates on all of the deeds you're holding.'

'Plus, there's also all of the new taxes we collected,' Baron joined in. 'When that new badge arrested Mike, he told him there would be a case against him for fraud. I don't have to tell you, Mike ain't gonna go to prison all by himself!'

Rutherford rubbed his temples, trying to think of a plan. The other two held their silence, because he was the leader, the man who made every key decision. He had never gotten them into a situation he couldn't handle; this would be no different.

'Baron,' he said, after a few moments of contemplation, 'you keep an eye on the goings-on at the jail. Let Mike know we won't let him stand before any judge. We've got a few days yet. All we have to do is get rid of those two troublemakers. And maybe,' he added, 'we'll also tend to the other guy who stuck his nose in this too.'

'Scraps is still out of any fight,' Baron warned. 'He's

got some cracked ribs and can hardly open his mouth wide enough for a spoonful of soup. The doc said it would take a month or more for him to heal. Mason actually fractured his jaw with one of his punches.' He shivered as if he had a cold chill. 'I told you, that guy hit harder than any man I ever seen.'

Dealer snorted his contempt. 'Yes, and your being too yellow to face him brought these two Valerons to town.'

Baron stiffened his back and hissed through his clenched teeth. 'I didn't hear you offering to take him on!'

'We hired you because you claimed to be a fast gun,' Dealer fired back. 'If you had killed Mason in a fair fight, no one would have blinked twice.'

'How was I supposed to know his relatives were a bunch of vengeance-seeking vigilantes?'

'Enough!' Rutherford commanded. 'We can't change what happened. They are here now and we have to deal with them. Baron, you get out there and keep an eye on those two lawmen. Make sure Mike gets the word to keep his mouth shut too.'

Baron glared at Dealer one last time, then left the room.

'Big talking blowhard,' Dealer spat out the words. 'Never did see him go up against anyone but a plowboy or wandering tramp. Bet he's never faced a real hard-case in his life.'

'We still need him . . . for the time being. Once this is behind us, we might want to trade up. I don't like the way he questions orders and then makes his own deci-sions. The act of cowardice – shooting Mason in the back

– is what put us in this hole.'

'What happens if the judge arrives before we get rid of those two?'

'We'll play this hand a while longer,' Rutherford suggested. 'I promise you one thing, no matter what the cost, not one of us is going to end up in prison!'

'Where are you taking my men?' Mike Lafferty protested the removal of Sandoval and Connor from the cell. 'It's almost midnight!'

'Stay quiet or you go hungry tomorrow!' Wyatt warned the man.

Lafferty muttered under his breath, as Wyatt and Jared bound the hands of the prisoners behind their backs and led them out into the night. Richard remained at the jail with his shotgun handy. He locked the door for security when the four of them left the office.

Outside, the small group made their way out of town and walked through the dark to the location Jared had selected. It was far enough away from the nearest house that a gunshot would not be heard over the music and raucous noise from the saloon.

Sandoval and Lafferty were both tough nuts and would be hard to crack, but Connor's picnic basket was short a sandwich or two. He would be their best chance to get a confession . . . if properly motivated.

'Game's over,' Wyatt spoke up, stopping inside the chaparral. The moonlight allowed the prisoners to see a small coulee, which had formed from rain and snow runoff at the base of three hills that came together at one edge of the cove. On all other sides was brush and cedar.

'What are we doing way out here?' Sandoval wanted to know.

Jared used an icy cold tone of voice. 'You're going to tell us what happened to the banker, or else you're going to wind up as coyote bait.'

'You can't do that!' Sandoval jeered, looking at Wyatt. 'You're wearing a badge!'

Wyatt displayed an insolent grin. 'I'm a local sheriff. I have no jurisdiction outside of Deliverance itself.' He purposely glanced around. 'Appears we're well outside of town.'

'You've got one chance to live,' Jared threatened. 'Tell us which of you shot our cousin in the back and who killed banker Walters. Next, you tell us where you buried the banker's body. Do that, and we won't leave you lying dead in the gully.'

Sandoval grunted his contempt. 'We ain't saying nothing.'

'Suit yourself,' Jared said. Then he proceeded to shove a rag in the man's mouth and secured it with a strip of cloth. Sandoval tried to curse them, but the gag muted his words so the sounds he made came out more like muffled oinks.

Wyatt took hold of Connor, as Jared led his partner over to the rim of the wash. Wyatt jerked Connor around to face him, getting right in his face.

'Your pal has made his choice,' Wyatt hissed menacingly. 'Time to make up your mind.'

'We don't know nothing!' the man blubbered, ducking his head to avoid Wyatt's dreadful glare.

Taking him by the shoulders, Wyatt spun him around, forcing him to look at Jared and Sandoval's dark forms. The two of them were standing at the rim of the gully, some fifty feet away. Even as they watched, Jared pulled his gun and pointed it at Connor's partner.

'Last chance,' Wyatt warned.

'I ain't got nothing to say.'

Jared called to Wyatt: 'He ready to talk?'

'No, he prefers to die too!' Wyatt replied.

Jared pointed his gun at Sandoval and pulled the trigger on his Colt!

The bound man crumbled to the ground and lay still. Jared holstered his weapon and callously used the toe of his boot to nudge the body over the edge of the wash. Then he walked calmly back to them.

'Did I hear right?' Jared had a simper on his lips. 'Is Connor ready to join his murdering pal?'

Connor began to tremble, his eyes rolled back and he shook his head fearfully.

'Well?' Wyatt demanded. 'You want to tell us what happened to Banker Walters, and who shot Mason, or do we shoot you too?'

The man held out, unwilling to talk ... until Jared took hold of his arm. 'Come on, loser,' he scoffed. 'I'm not going to drag your lifeless body all the way over to the coulee.'

'No! Wait!' he wailed, digging in his heels. 'Me and Sandoval didn't kill nobody, see? We only did what we was told.'

'And what was that?' Wyatt prodded.

'Baron was the one who shot Mason!' Connor cried,

nearly babbling with terror. 'He's also killed Walters. Me and Sandoval only buried the banker's body. That's all we done. I swear, we never kilt no one!'

'Who gave the order to kill the banker?'

'Dealer and Rutherford give all of the orders. Baron and Mike does what they say, and me and Sandoval do what Mike tells us to.'

'Where did you bury the body?' Jared asked.

'Yonder,' Connor replied, tipping his head back in the direction of town. 'Not far from the cemetery, in an empty field.'

Jared ordered: 'You lead us to the spot – right now. If you're lying to us, we'll come back here and leave your dead carcass to rot alongside your partner. You hear me?'

Connor bobbed his head up and down, then started off down the trail they had used. He was walking fast, hurrying, as if running for his life.

Soon as the two were moveing away, Wyatt called to Landau: 'You can get up now and take Sandoval back to the cell!'

The man appeared, rubbing a tender spot on his ribs. 'Jared like to stuck his toe right through me. Next time, he can pretend to get shot!'

Baron appeared at the house as Dealer and Rutherford were getting ready for breakfast. He didn't bother to knock, walking in unannounced.

'We're treading deep water now,' he told them both. 'Those lawmen found the banker's body.'

'What?' Rutherford yelped. 'How the hell—'

'Connor,' was the single word he used to cut off the question.

Dealer swore. 'How did that happen? The man was in the same cell with Lafferty and Sandoval. He knew to keep his mouth shut.'

Baron explained: 'Some kind of trick, I think.' Then he explained how he had seen the two Valeron boys take Sandoval and Connor out of the jail. He hadn't dared follow them in the dark and maybe give himself away. 'I heard a single shot a short while later,' he went on with his story, 'and thought one of our boys might have tried something.'

'So what did happen?'

'After a few minutes, I see some joker – looked like the same guy Bernie knew, the one who helped against Markum's men. Anyway, he was herding Sandoval back to the jail. A half-hour or so later, Connor and the two lawmen show up. It was strange as could be. Anyway, I slipped over to check where I'd had them bury Walters and, sure enough, his body was lying there next to a hole. I was almost seen, because one of the Valeron boys and the Brooks guy showed up. They carted the banker's body off toward the doctor's place.'

'That tears it,' Dealer said. 'We've got to pack up, grab what money we can, and set fire to our horses' tails!'

'What about Lafferty?' Baron wanted to know. 'He'll crow like a rooster at first light if we leave him behind. That means having our faces on wanted posters all over Colorado!'

Rutherford was thoughtful for a full minute. When he spoke, he had a crooked smirk on his lips. 'Remember how we handled this same type of situation in Cactus Creek?'

'Yeah,' Dealer replied. 'But we had half-dozen other men with us. With Lafferty and his boys locked up, there's only four of us left . . . and Scraps ain't up to any kind of fight.'

'There are six men sitting in jail,' Rutherford reminded him. 'I've an idea how to spring them all, kill the Valerons, and take every dime from this town. We'll be able to start over anywhere we please.'

'I'm listening,' Dealer said. 'You've always figured a way out before. You tell us what to do and we'll get it done.'

'Count me in too,' Baron joined in. 'What's the plan?'

CHAPTER TEN

'Dad-gum!' Shane blurted unhappily. 'Look where we are!' He laughed without mirth. 'We could have had a nice warm bed and a hot meal last night.'

Cliff groaned. 'Ain't that the truth! We weren't but a couple miles from Deliverance, only we didn't know it.'

'Yeah, I've never been here before and had no idea how far we'd come in the dark. Besides, it was near midnight when we camped for the night.'

'Five more minutes,' Cliff continued to gripe. 'Maybe one more hill, and we'd have seen the lights from town.'

'Good thing we didn't waste time fixing breakfast. We can hit the café first thing and get a good meal. Then we can find your brother and our cousins.'

'This is how it ought to be,' Cliff said. 'One member from each of our families – well, at least all three Valeron families, along with us Masons.'

'Unbeatable combination,' Shane agreed. 'Let's mosey on down and strap on the feedbag.'

'I'm with you,' Cliff said. 'I'm hungry enough to eat my own cooking!'

Shane chuckled. 'Thankfully, I've never been that hungry.'

Landau had been on watch all night, so Richard relieved him at first light. Jared and Wyatt had spent the night in Landau's room, as they were both in dire need of sleep. Their first stop was to visit Julia's to see if there was a bullet to be found in the banker's body. If so, did it match the one from Rod Mason's back? That would tie the two shootings together – added proof for a judge, as to who the shooter was.

'Long night,' Landau welcomed Richard. 'You keep the shotgun handy. Wyatt thinks Rudy's Renegades might pull something today. They are running out of time.'

'I'll keep the door locked,' Richard promised. 'You better get a couple hours sleep, in case there is some trouble.'

Landau left the jail and headed for the hotel. Richard was watching as the two Valeron cousins appeared on the street. The three of them stopped to talk for a minute, then Landau continued off toward the hotel, while Wyatt and Jared made their way to the doctor's house.

Richard felt a tingle of apprehension. He was involved in an adventure beyond anything he had ever imagined. His entire adult life had been spent looking over account books, ledgers, and counting other people's money. Before Lynette's cry for help had rocked his world, he had been solitary, living like a hermit, a mousy sort of person to all who knew him. Since joining up with Mason, he had been in a fight, nearly kidnapped, and was now guarding six outlaws by himself. He wondered: *Am I more of a man now? Or am I risking my life for nothing more than the male ego?*

'When's breakfast, Glasses?' Sandoval demanded to know.

Richard turned to look at him. 'I only wear spectacles when I'm working on a journal or tallying figures. If you wish to get fed today, you will refrain from calling me names.'

The man pulled a face. 'Durned if you ain't starting to sound like one of them Valerons.'

Rotating about to keep watch out the barred front window of the office, Richard hid the smile that came to his lips. He found Sandoval's comment to be a compliment, and it felt . . . good.

'What do you think?' Wyatt asked Julia. 'Are they the same?'

The doctor had a small scale and had placed each slug on it to get a reading. She rose up, putting her hands to the small of her back and stretched from having been bending over for several minutes.

'The size and weight are the same,' she announced. 'That doesn't mean both bullets came from the same gun, but it does mean the gun used was the same caliber.'

'It will be good enough,' Jared said. 'We know Baron is the man who pulled the trigger.'

'Is there anything else we can use?' Wyatt asked her. 'Anything you can tell about the body that might give us more evidence?'

'Mort Walters was in his night clothes, meaning whoever killed him probably dragged him from his bedroom.'

'Yeah,' Wyatt agreed. 'We didn't even find any shoes. This was about as cold-blooded as any murder I've ever seen.'

'Shooting Mr Mason in the back was equally cold-blooded,' Julia said. 'Any word on when to expect the circuit judge?'

'Two or three days, according to Landau,' Jared was the one to answer. 'The judge had one case to hear at Fairfield before he headed our way.'

Julia took a moment to study the two Valerons. 'You know Rutherford will have to act. He won't wait around to stand trial. You've gathered too much evidence against him.'

'We are taking every precaution possible,' Wyatt responded. 'Now that we know the bullets were likely from the same gun, we can make an arrest or two.'

'You're out of room at the jail. Where are you going to put any more prisoners?'

Jared raised his hand like he was in a classroom. 'We can hang three or four of them? That would make room for new arrests.'

Julia fixed a quizzical look on Wyatt. 'Did this character ever meet an outlaw he didn't want to hang?'

'No, ma'am,' Wyatt replied. 'Not to my knowledge.'

Richard was sitting behind the desk when he heard a rush of footsteps come up to the bolted door. There came a sudden rapping, followed by a panicked voice.

'Open up, Sheriff! Hurry!'

Richard went to the window and peeked out. It was Dealer Gilmore. He didn't appear to be wearing a gun, but was looking around expectantly, as if he thought someone would be watching or following.

Picking up the shotgun, Richard unbolted the door and opened it a few inches. 'What's the trouble?'

'It's Baron and Rudy!' Dealer gasped the words. 'They are going to grab your sister. I tried to talk them out of it, but they're running scared.'

The news shocked Richard. 'Why would they take Lynette?'

'For security. They are going to keep her hostage until they get out of the country.'

Richard frowned. 'I thought you and Rutherford were in this together?'

'You remember my shooting one of the Barkley brothers? The one who had you by the collar?' Dealer grunted. 'Well, that kind of ended our friendship. Rutherford is the one who put them up to kidnapping you!'

'The Valerons are over at the doctor's house,' Richard told him.

'There's no time to waste!' Dealer said, looking around nervously. 'They wouldn't believe me. You'll have to tell them!'

'But I can't leave the jail.'

Dealer hesitated but a moment. 'I'll watch the jail. You have to save your sister. I've loved her since I met her,' he confessed. 'But Rudy holds her responsible for everything that's gone wrong. He won't ever let her go.

147

If they take her with them, they will kill her!'

Richard didn't know what to do. He had promised to guard the jail. But his sister was in danger; she might be fighting for her life at this very moment.

'All right!' Richard gave in. 'You bolt the door and wait for me or Wyatt. I'll go alert them and hope we're in time to save my sister!' Pushing past Dealer, he took the scatter-gun and darted off toward Julia's place.

'Hurry!' Dealer called to his back. 'Don't let them take Lynette!'

Richard burst through the mayor's door to see Julia and the two Valeron boys. They were standing near the covered body of the banker. He practically ranted the story of how Lynette was in danger. Seconds later, the three of them were making their way to the newspaper office.

Jared went through an alley so he could come in from a different direction. Wyatt and Richard approached cautiously from the front. There was no sign of life as they approached the office door.

'Looks quiet,' Wyatt whispered to Richard. 'Keep the shotgun handy.'

Jared came from the back, panting from the strenuous run. 'Nothing!' he gasped. 'And no one moving around at the livery, not that I could see.'

Richard tested the front door. It was locked, but it was still an hour before opening time. He put his knuckles to the wood, knocking loudly. After a few moments, both Mason and Lynette appeared on the stairway at the back of the room. It was Lynette who hurried over to open the door for them.

148

'What is it?' she asked, immediately concerned.

'Anything wrong?' Richard asked. 'Anyone try to get inside in the past few minutes?'

'No,' Lynette replied. 'I was having breakfast with Rodney.'

Jared uttered an intentional grunt. 'Tell us again, Brooks. Who did you leave in charge of the jail?'

'Dealer said he'd had a falling out with Rutherford, due to his killing one of the Barkley boys.'

Wyatt sighed. 'Except we know he only fired on the kidnappers to keep them from telling who had hired them. Dealer was protecting himself.'

Jared eased out of the office far enough to look up the street. The front door to the jail was open and men were filing out, all of them armed.

'Looks like a major jailbreak taking place, Cuz,' he spoke to Wyatt. 'I'd guess this was the plan – get Richard out of the way and turn loose the prisoners.'

'I'm in this with you this time,' Mason spoke up. 'Lynette, get me my gun.'

The lady gave him a loving gaze. 'I know you have to do this, Rodney,' she murmured. 'I'll help you, but don't you dare get yourself killed!'

'I promise,' he said. Then as she swiftly went up the stairs, he turned toward Wyatt. 'Where is Landau?'

'Room number seven at the hotel. You go get him and meet us out in the street. We'll try and slow down Rutherford and his men.'

'Has everyone got a gun?' Dealer asked. 'We don't have much time.'

Rutherford snorted his contempt. 'What can two or three men do against all of us? If the Valerons take us on, we'll leave them lying in the street, face down in a pool of their own blood.'

'Don't look like they are all that scart of us,' Connor sounded off. 'Yonder they is and they're headed this way.'

Rutherford moved up next to Dealer. His partner heaved a sigh. 'We should have grabbed the money and had the horses ready. I didn't want to have to deal with them.'

'Two men and a banker,' Rutherford dismissed his concern.

'That banker is packing a 10-gauge scatter-gun,' Baron spoke up from behind the two of them. 'And Wyatt Valeron is 'bout the most dangerous gunman in this part of the country.'

Rutherford was smug. 'There are ten of us. He'd be a complete fool to take on such long odds.'

'They sure enough look like they mean business,' Sandoval put in.

'I'm not eager for a gunfight,' Lafferty muttered.

'You'll stand with the rest of us,' Rutherford warned, 'or else we'll leave you in one of the jail cells.'

'Everyone get ready,' Dealer told the group of men. 'No one get too eager to fire his gun. We might be able to talk our way through this without any killing.'

'I never agreed to that!' Rutherford sounded off.

'Yeah, well I don't want to be looking over my shoulder for the rest of my life. If we kill those two Valerons, their kin will hunt us forever.'

'All right,' Rutherford conceded. 'We'll try it your way first. If you fail, we mow down the three of them and walk over their dead bodies on our way to get our money and pick up the horses.'

'Fan out, men,' Dealer ordered, moving out to confront Wyatt and his two men.

Wyatt and Jared slowed to a stop, fifty feet away, as an uneven skirmish line of outlaws formed opposite of them. Wyatt moved one step closer, taking up the position of spokesman. Dealer had already done the same. Every man had their hand on the butt of their gun, all of them primed for a fight.

'I'm asking you men to throw down your weapons,' Wyatt said in a clear voice. 'Rutherford, Baron and Dealer, you three are under arrest for the murder of Mort Walters. Surrender your guns; we don't want a lot of dead bodies today.'

'You are holding a pair of deuces in a jacks-or-better game of cards, Sheriff,' Dealer replied with a mocking simper. 'What can you do against so many of us?'

'First off,' Wyatt ignored the question, pausing to evaluate the string of men. 'Scraps,' he spoke to the big man. 'I'm told you have sore ribs and a fractured jaw. I don't believe you want to try pulling and firing a gun. The sudden movement would put you on your knees.'

Dealer laughed at the observation. 'He's right, Scraps. Drop your pistol and step over to the porch. We don't need your gun.'

The large brute unhitched his gunbelt and let it fall to the ground. Then he lumbered a few steps away to be out of the line of fire.

'How about you two, Sandoval and Connor?' Wyatt targeted the pair. 'You boys are only looking at a few months' time in jail for covering up a murder. Do you really want the law after you for killing a sheriff?'

There was no humour on Dealer's face this time. 'You men work for us!' he snarled at them. 'If this comes to gunplay, you'll do your part and shoot to kill. There's nine of us and only three of them. We can—'

'Best count again,' a voice called out, cutting him short.

All attention went to the walkway leading to the hotel. Rod Mason and Landau were approaching, both armed and ready to fight.

'Mason?' Dealer was aghast. 'How the hell—?'

'There are still only five of them!' Rutherford asserted, moving up to side Dealer. 'We've still got two-to-one odds in our favour.'

Mason and Landau kept coming until they joined up with Wyatt, then Landau spoke up.

'Got word from the authorities down in Texas,' he announced. 'Rudy's Renegades are wanted for murder, extortion and numerous other crimes. The warrants name all five men: Rutherford, Gilmore, Lafferty, Baron and Scraps.'

'Sounds as if a noose is waiting for each of them,' Jared said. 'Are the rest of you willing to die to protect them?'

'Don't listen to their lies!' Rutherford shouted to his group.

'Then listen to this!' Wyatt retorted. With a deadly

gaze, he purposely examined the faces of every man in the group. 'I can kill two of you before you get off a shot, possibly a third man as well,' he coolly assessed. 'Jared here will also take a man or two with him. Lightning Rod Mason has beaten two men in a gunfight before, so add that into the mix. As for Landau, he's nearly as good as Jared – which means he'll get another one or two of you before he goes down. Brooks here has a shotgun and he'll fire both loads into your line. I figure his buckshot will kill at least one man and maybe wing a couple more.'

Wyatt gave his head a negative shake. 'Way I see it, if this comes to a shootout, every man-jack of you will end up dead or dying on the street.'

'He's bluffing, men!' Rutherford growled. 'We are nine guns to their five. They have no chance against us if we stick together!'

His declaration was followed by a stressful few moments in time. Stillness, quietude, the air barely stirring with a slight morning breeze. Every man was primed to kill or be killed. Hearts pounded with anticipation and nerves were strained to breaking point. One hiccup, a deep breath – anything could signal the start of a bloody battle.

Abruptly, the sound of two horses approaching broke the tense moment. Everyone's attention was averted to a pair of riders. They continued right up to the squared-off units, not stopping until they were next to Wyatt's position. Purposely, the two turned their horses to face Rutherford's gang.

'I reckon you need to tally the numbers one more time,' Wyatt said, displaying a confident grin. 'These are my cousins, Shane Valeron and Rod Mason's brother, Cliff. If my count is correct, that makes the reckoning seven to nine.'

The two climbed down from their horses and moved to stand alongside Wyatt's group. Both were young, but they were packing iron and appeared capable.

Wyatt took advantage of the doubt he saw on some of the faces of Rutherford's men. 'What about it, Sandoval? Last chance for you and Connor to survive this. Do you want to die for the simple crime of burying a body?'

Sandoval lifted his hands up, palms out and backed up a step. 'No way,' he said. 'Me and Connor are out of this.' Giving a signal to Connor, they both dropped their guns.

'Stand over with Scraps,' Wyatt ordered.

Rutherford couldn't believe it. He swallowed hard and looked around. The numbers were now even – seven on each side. And he and Dealer were not gunmen. They had always hired others to do their fighting for them. Before he could get his brain working, Jared directed a challenge to Markum's three remaining gang members.

'How about you boys?' he asked the trio. 'Are you ready to die for Rutherford and Dealer?'

The one who had surrendered during Markum's failed ambush replied. 'We ain't never done no killin',' he said. 'We rustled a few head of cattle – that's all.'

'Time to decide if you want to spend a year or two behind bars or end up dead,' Jared said. 'No way any of you survive if this comes to gunplay.'

The one looked at his two companions. At his nod, all

three loosened their gunbelts and let them fall. 'We're out of it,' he said. 'We'll be in our cell.'

Even as Rutherford was cursing their cowardice, the three men walked back to the jail.

Now faced with unbeatable odds, Lafferty threw up his hands.

'It wasn't me who gave the orders to kill the banker or shoot Mason in the back!' he cried. 'Rudy and Dealer – they told Baron to do those jobs. Baron's the one who did the killing!'

Baron swore and spun on the ex-mayor. 'You big-mouth, yella' dog!' he snarled. Then, without warning, he drew his gun and pulled the trigger, drilling Lafferty in the chest!

Wyatt and Rod Mason reacted instantly, both men firing with deadly accuracy. Baron was hit twice and sank to his knees. As his gun slipped from his fingers, he fell alongside Lafferty, both of them stone-dead, sprawled together on the dusty street.

Jared and Landau had also pulled their guns, but Dealer and Rutherford weren't about to test their skill against the sheriff or his men. Slowly, deliberately, the two remaining outlaws lifted their hands in defeat.

'Put them four to a cell, Deputy,' Wyatt instructed Jared. 'Brooks, you keep them covered with your shotgun until they are safely locked away.'

Jared waved his gun to start the pair walking. 'By Jingo!' he said happily. 'Looks like we have a couple left to hang.'

Brooks gathered up Sandoval, Connor and Scraps, and they all filed into the sheriff's office.

Soon as they were off the street, Shane grinned broadly and stuck out his hand to Wyatt. 'Looks like Cliff and I arrived in the nick of time,' he said.

'Good thing Rutherford and his men didn't come out shooting,' Rod commented, moving over to join them, 'or you'd have got here too late.'

'Me and Shane had the town in our sights,' Cliff spoke up. 'We'd have come in like twin tornadoes if a gunfight had started.'

'Well, I'm durn glad you made it when you did,' Landau joined the group. 'I don't mind telling you, I was sweating blood for a time. That little standoff cost me five years of my life.'

'Funny, you don't look no older,' Shane quipped. 'You're what – thirty-eight or -nine?'

Landau grunted. 'I take it back – we were doing fine without you two.'

Cliff came forward to shake hands with his brother. Then he stepped back and looked him over. 'You don't look any worse for having been shot in the back.'

'Only hurts when I laugh,' Rod said. 'If you start telling us again about saving all of our lives, it'd plumb buckle me in the middle.'

'You too?' Cliff wailed. 'All I get from the Valerons is flack about this or that. I swear, if it wasn't for being responsible for taking care of Nessy, I'd ride off and never look back.'

'Shucks, Clifford,' Wyatt told him, seriously. 'You know we only rib you because we like you.'

Jared added: 'Sure, it's almost as if you're one of the family.'

'Besides that,' Shane concluded, 'it isn't your fault that you're such an easy target. You were pretty much born that way.'

Cliff pulled a face. 'Thanks a lot.'

'Wyatt,' Shane chortled. 'Wait'll you hear about the great deal Cliff made with Tish. I tell you, my little sister ought to become a lawyer or politician. She can wheel and deal like no one else on the ranch.'

'Maybe later,' Wyatt gave Cliff a reprieve from the teasing. 'You two put up your horses; Rod, you get back to bed; and we'll all get together in an hour or so to decide what needs to be done here in town.'

'I'll tend to these two bodies,' Landau offered. 'Soon as I get a couple men to help get them off the street, I'll join Shane at the livery. We need to check on our livestock and figure what to do with any extra mounts.'

'I've got to talk to the mayor,' Wyatt said. 'She will want to be a part of our conference.'

Rod spoke up. 'I'll inform Lynette Brooks. She'll want to be there too. She's the town editor. Whatever we decide, she can make it public in a special edition of her newspaper.'

'Everyone figure on meeting at the saloon in one hour,' Wyatt outlined. 'Shane, you and Cliff will watch the prisoners during our meeting, because you aren't up to date on what all is going on.'

'Right,' Shane agreed. 'We'll see to it that no one gets out of line.'

Mason walked through the entrance way of the newspaper office and right into Lynette's arms. She hugged him for a long time, before finally leaning back enough to kiss him. When she stood back, Mason saw tears in her eyes.

'It's over,' he told her gently. 'Rutherford and the others are in jail.'

'When I heard shooting, I was—'

Mason bent down and kissed her. 'It's over,' he assured her a second time.

'What will happen now?'

'Wyatt is setting up a meeting. You are to be there, along with the mayor, your brother, and the rest of us. Everything will be ironed out and you will have a major story to write.'

A smile came to her lips. 'I didn't tell you, because I was afraid something might go wrong.'

'Tell me what?'

'Well, from the time you arrived, I started sending my editorials to the *Rocky Mountain News* in Denver. They not only published my last three articles, they are going to buy everything I write. As some of their news is also picked up by newspaper outlets back east, I will make more selling them what I write than I will on local sales and advertising.'

'That's great!' Mason praised. 'You're a success.'

Lynette put her hands up to his face, brushing his cheeks as she slipped her fingers around behind his neck. Her features were soft and inviting, her eyes glowing with enchantment and desire.

'Mason,' she whispered huskily, 'I want us to be together. When the shots rang out, I nearly died, fearful you would never return.'

'I'm here,' he said, as tenderly as his deep voice would allow. 'And I'm not going anywhere.'

'Do you think you could be satisfied to set print and help me run this newspaper?'

He didn't answer in words, he pulled her into his arms and explained it with his actions.

Shane and Cliff stopped atop a knoll and took a moment to look back at Deliverance.

'I wish we could stick around for the trial,' Shane said. 'I'm curious as to how much time some of those boys will serve.'

Cliff remarked: 'Jared figures Rutherford and Dealer will hang. That ought to suit him.'

'A lot of changes are going to take place. Richard is moving to Deliverance – taking possession of the dead banker's house – and will assume running the bank. He's going to keep the housekeeper and make everything right concerning the crooked interest rates. Then Landau is helping Bernie to take over the saloon. He is going to use whatever excess money there is to pay back the high taxes the other businesses have paid out.'

'And Wyatt will have to find a good man to take over as sheriff. He said Julia knew of a ranch hand who had been a deputy once. He'll probably stick around long enough to show the guy the ropes.'

'As for me, I'd have liked to see my brother up to his elbows in ink.' Cliff laughed. 'I'll bet his hands are blue for the wedding next month.'

'Reckon you can pay Tish to watch Nessy when we return for the blissful event.'

'No way,' Cliff was adamant. 'I'll bring my girl along with me in one of the carriages from the ranch. I can't afford your sister's rates.'

'Let's kick up some dust,' Shane said. 'We've a long ride ahead of us.'

'I'm with you, Cuz. Let's make tracks for home!'